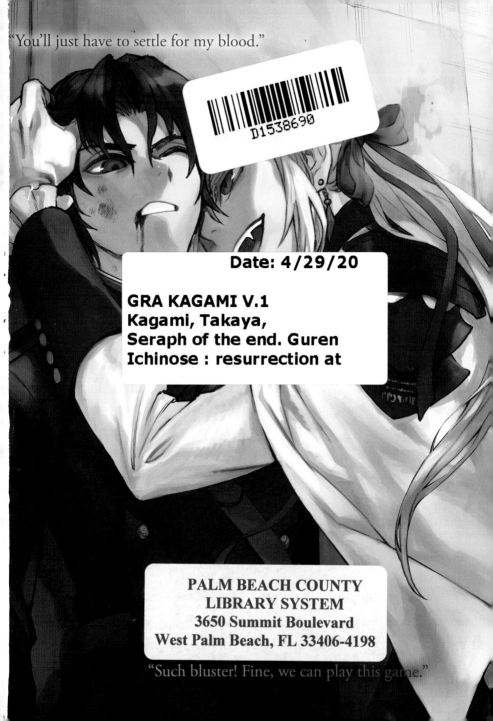

"You'll just have to settle for my blood."

Date: 4/29/20

GRA KAGAMI V.1
Kagami, Takaya,
Seraph of the end. Guren
Ichinose : resurrection at

"Such bluster! Fine, we can play this game."

This was the last time he would ever have the privilege of crying.

"WAAAAAAAAAAAAAAAAAAAAAAAAAAA
AAAAAAAAA!"

He howled, beating his fists against the earth, choking on his own despair.

His cries echoed across the beautiful night sky. But there was no one left to hear him.

Everyone was dead.

And Guren had killed them.

CONTENTS

Seraph of the End

Guren Ichinose: Resurrection at Nineteen

1

Story by Takaya Kagami
Art by Yo Asami

Translated by James Balzer

VERTICAL.

Seraph of the End
Guren Ichinose: Resurrection at Nineteen 1

Editor: Daniel Joseph

Art by Yo Asami.

Originally published in Japanese as
Owari no Serafu - Ichinose Guren, 19-sai no Sekaisaitan 1.

This is a work of fiction.

ISBN: 978-1-949980-05-9

Manufactured in the United States of America

First Edition

Kodansha USA Publishing, LLC.
451 Park Avenue South
7th Floor
New York, NY 10016
www.vertical-inc.com

Seraph of the End

Guren Ichinose: Resurrection at Nineteen

1

"Hey, Guren. Guren."

"…"

"Hey, Guren."

"What the hell do you want?"

"You been getting horny at all lately?"

"What…?!" What kind of a question was that? Guren Ichinose shot an exasperated glance at the boy crouched next to him, who was staring intently through the scope of his rifle.

The boy was Shinya Hiragi.

Shinya was sixteen years old, the same age as Guren. He had white hair, and was dressed in a combat uniform. He did not return Guren's glance. They were in the middle of a mission, and Shinya had to keep his eyes trained on his scope.

"So you haven't?" persisted Shinya, never looking away from his rifle.

"Haven't what??"

"Been getting horny."

"Why the hell are we even talking about this?"

"Well, you're the one who brought it up," replied Shinya.

Which was news to Guren. "When did I bring it up?" he asked, cocking his head in confusion.

"Just now."

"No I didn't!"

"Yes you did."

"No I didn't! That is, I wouldn't! This is no time to be talking about something like that," insisted Guren, his eyes fixed on the window.

They were stationed on one of the upper floors of an abandoned building. And they were on an important mission, which is why they couldn't take their eyes off that window, even for a second.

Nevertheless, Shinya pressed on.

"Well? Have you?"

"Drop it already."

"Been getting horny."

"Why the hell do you want to talk about this right now?"

"You prefer porno mags? Or do you like videos better?"

"Concentrate on the mission, Shinya."

"Come on, tell me! Videos or magazines?"

"Hmph… How about you tell me, which do you prefer?"

"Me…? That's a tough one. They've both got their charms, wouldn't you say?"

"How the hell should I know?"

"Hahaha," Shinya laughed, but his eyes never moved from the scope of his rifle.

The two of them had been staring out the window for four hours at this point.

They were keeping watch.

If they saw anyone coming from the west on the street below, it was Guren and Shinya's job to stop them.

Their friends were currently in the basement of that same building, working feverishly to save the world.

More specifically, they were trying to restore power to the area, though why it was so important to get the power back on is a story for another time.

All that mattered right now was keeping watch over that street.

Would the enemy appear?

Would someone try to interfere?

But four hours is a long time to keep watch, so naturally they started shooting the shit while they waited.

Mostly they stuck to small talk—video games, the weather, sports (though when it came down to it, neither of the boys actually knew a thing about sports). Just pointless small talk.

Regardless, Guren couldn't recall either of them bringing up sex.

In which case…

"Shinya?"

"Yeah?"

"What was I talking about that could possibly have anything to do with sex?"

"You brought up the weather, didn't you?" replied Shinya breezily.

"Sure."

"And it's sunny today."

"Uh huh."

"It's so beautiful out, but nearly everyone is dead. The world has ended. It's all pretty bleak, isn't it?"

"…"

"And then you were saying that in a world like this, it's hard to know what's right anymore. You were worried that life has lost its meaning."

"Yeah, I remember."

Outside, the sky was clear.

The bright rays of the sun beat down silently. It was almost oppressively peaceful.

Shinya went on. "So, I started thinking…"

"…"

"…about what it means to be alive. What's the point? What meaning *does* life have in a world like this?"

"And…?"

"And I pretty much came up empty… But I figure getting horny, that's something. That gives life some kind of meaning."

"…"

"Well, maybe not meaning, but at least it shows you've still got the will to live. You get horny because some part of you refuses to give up on life. Same reason you get hungry, probably, or sleepy. Your belly is empty, you think dirty thoughts, you close your eyes because you're so damn tired."

"That's just called being a dumb oaf."

"Hahaha, but that's just it, isn't it?" said Shinya. "I figure the body's just a big, dumb, optimistic oaf. All it wants to do is live."

So physiological appetites prove the will to live. And yet…

"Does life have meaning just because the body is alive?"

"I wonder."

"Is there really a right answer in a world like this?"

Shinya shrugged. "Were you always of the opinion that only the righteous deserve to live?"

"…"

"Or are you taking your cues from someone else about what it means to be right?"

"No… I mean yes, but… Maybe talking to you about it would make me feel better."

Guren could feel Shinya smiling beside him.

"That's why I brought it up. You looked like there was something you needed to get off your chest. So?"

"What?"

"What is it that's bothering you?"

"…"

"Is it that you're worried life has no meaning in a world like this?"

"…Well, does it? What do you think?"

"Hmm," Shinya replied, screwing up his face. "I mean, I'm not sure life had meaning even before all this."

True, Shinya's world had been a grim one indeed. He had been sold off as a child and spent his whole life in training, solely so he could serve as Mahiru Hiragi's fiancé.

Shinya spent his childhood in a place where those who were weak, those who didn't serve a purpose, were quickly disposed of.

The fact that he had survived to stand here today meant that he, too, must have killed his share.

So Shinya must have given plenty of thought to the meaning of life. Why go on? What was it all for?

But of course these were no easy questions to answer.

And now, on top of everything else, the world had come to an end.

Humankind had fallen from its former glory, even losing their place at the top of the food chain.

What meaning could life have in a world like that?

"…"

"…"

The two fell silent for a moment then, simply staring out at the lifeless city.

Without anyone to run the power station, the electrical grid had gone down. Once the sun set, the city would be enveloped in a pitch-black night.

A few minutes passed before Guren spoke again. "With things the way they are, is there really any point to living?"

"Guren," replied Shinya.

"Yeah?"

"Don't ask me."

"Fair enough."

"I'll tell you what, if you say there's still meaning to life, then I'll say there is, too."

"Chickenshit."

But Shinya just laughed. "Well, make up your mind, Guren. Does life have meaning or not?"

"..."

"Come on, which is it? If it doesn't, I'm gonna off myself, so hurry up and decide already," Shinya said with a shit-eating grin that implied the answer was a no-brainer: it seemed pretty clear he expected Guren to say life had meaning.

"..."

But did it? Guren frowned.

Was there really any point to living in a world like this?

To being dragged back from the dead—and forced to live in a world like this?

There was no answer to that question. Or at least no correct answer, nothing you could call right in any sense of the word.

But Guren answered anyway. "It does."

"Yeah?"

"Yes, life has meaning."

"That's your decision?"

"Yup, that's my decision."

"It's settled then. So you don't need to worry about it anymore, right?"

"Yeah."

"And who do you have to thank for that?" coaxed Shinya.

Before Guren could respond, however—

Movement! Guren spotted someone outside, coming from the west.

It was a vampire.

Almost all the humans were gone; the only ones who could walk around in the open like that now were vampires and monsters.

"We've got incoming," said Guren, his gaze fixed on the figure in the distance.

Shinya nodded. "I see him. I think I can pick him off from here—"

"You'll never hit him at this distance. Those creatures are too powerful."

"You're probably right."

"I'm going out there. I'll pin him down, you take the kill."

"Gotcha. And Guren?"

"Yeah?"

"Remember, life has meaning. It's got to. So don't go getting yourself killed."

Guren nodded and drew the sword he wore at his waist.

The fight for survival was about to begin.

Seraph of the End

But this story begins a little earlier.
At the moment the world came to an end.

This is a story of the first days after the fall—

Rape, for instance, is a sin, is it not?

Imagine a man forces himself upon a woman, devastates her physically and mentally. Perhaps the woman commits suicide afterward, and her family is left with nothing but grief and lamentation.

It's the worst thing imaginable. Horrible even to contemplate.

And yet it happens all the time, it's a story that has repeated itself again and again across the years, even as humankind has grown and prospered.

A crime against all morality—and yet, God has not sat in judgment on this sin.

What of violence and murder, then? Are these sins?

Is it a sin to kill an insect?

An animal?

A person?

Are some lives worth more than others? Are some sins, in turn, weightier than others? Humans have killed their fellows. They have killed animals and eaten them. Some have even killed and eaten other humans. And yet these stories, too, have repeated themselves again and again throughout history, each more common than the last.

There are those who have cried out that such sins are unforgivable—and yet no divine punishment has been handed down.

What is a sin, then?
What sin could be unforgivable?
The Tower of Babel?
Icarus?
Of the great and sundry sins of this world, what transgression could be so taboo as to be truly beyond redemption?

"..."

Guren Ichinose had committed a grievous sin.
An unpardonable sin.
He had violated a taboo, committed a transgression against the universe.
Who knew what god it had angered, or if there even was a god to anger.
But there had been punishment.
There had been a fall.

Humankind's prosperity had met its end.

"Why, dammit, why?!" Guren screamed.

He was in Shinjuku, deep underground, screaming within the bowels of the earth.

"Why, goddammit, why?! Why won't you come back?!"

Seven coffins stood in a row. Guren was screaming as he stared into the one he had just opened.

A miracle had occurred in six of the seven coffins.

The dead had returned to life.

Their heads, severed from their bodies, had reattached themselves, and now there they lay, cheeks rosy and hearts beating as if nothing had ever happened.

The coffins housed his friends, his family—Norito, Mito, Sayuri, Shigure—as well as two men he had never seen before, and all six were starting to revive.

Four friends and two strangers. They slept peacefully, seemingly oblivious to the fact that just moments before they had been dead.

But in the seventh coffin…

"Why won't you come back to life?! You're supposed to come back!" Guren shouted, pounding on the chest of his friend. The only one of the seven who remained lifeless.

Guren Ichinose: Resurrection at Nineteen

"Come back!" Guren shouted, as he tried in vain to restart the unbeating heart of his friend Shinya Hiragi.

"Wake up! Come back! Please!"

But Shinya's heart refused to beat.

He wasn't breathing.

His wounds had closed, including the gaping hole in his chest—the one that had killed him. But for some reason he wouldn't wake up.

"Shinya! Shinya!" Guren shouted, but Shinya's eyes remained closed.

"Shinya! Wake up! Open your eyes!"

Guren shook him.

He beat at his chest.

He pleaded.

"You're supposed to come back! That was the deal!" Guren screamed. "Who?! Who'll bring him back?! God?! The devil?! Anyone?! I broke the taboo! Accept it! I'll take the punishment! I'll take any punishment you can think of! Just bring Shinya back!"

He prayed thus to God, his eyes turned heavenward.

But there was no reply.

Not from God, anyway.

Elsewhere, however, a voice spoke. It issued from within the sprawling, underground laboratory. The voice of a capricious man who had come to gawp at the foolish sins of humankind—

"Odd, he should have come back to life. Maybe this one didn't take," the man mused aloud as he approached.

He was terribly beautiful, with long, silver hair.

Red eyes.

Razor-sharp fangs.

He was a vampire.

And a noble at that.

The man who called himself Ferid Bathory took his time as he approached Guren.

And looking down at the lifeless body of Shinya, he smiled. "Mmm, see how beautiful his face looks in death. It would almost be a shame to bring this one back..."

"Shut your mouth, bloodsucker!"

"Oh my, how fearsome. But I've never once shut this mouth, not since the day I was born. My dear papa and mama always told me I'd been running my filthy mouth since the moment I crawled from my mother's loins. Hmm, hold on now. Were those my parents? No? Maybe? Who can say. Well, no matter—" Ferid broke off, grinning. "Either way, I'm afraid I won't be taking orders from you, boy."

Ferid stretched out a hand toward Shinya.

Guren grabbed his arm. "Don't touch him."

"Why not? It's already dead."

"I'm going to bring him back. That's why I—"

"Why you violated the taboo?"

"..."

Yes. It was true. He had carried out an unconscionable experiment. One that the vampires had done everything in their power to prevent.

The resurrection of a human being.

It was an unforgivable sin. But whom did it anger? And why must there be punishment? Guren had no idea.

According to Mahiru, however, bringing back the dead would set the end in motion.

The end of the world.

Only children and demons would survive, and the population

would be reduced to less than one tenth of what it had been.

Not to mention the fact that, despite paying such a hefty price, those who were brought back in this way would be brought back incomplete, with but ten more years to live.

"…"

And Guren had no idea if what she had said was even true.

They were still underground. Isolated from the world.

For all Guren knew, the world outside really had ended.

Or maybe it had all been a lie conjured up by Mahiru, and nothing had happened at all. Maybe the resurrection procedure had been a success, and there was no punishment after all.

Guren didn't care. He had made his decision regardless of whether or not it would invite divine punishment. It didn't matter if it was only ten years, he just wanted to spend that time with his family and friends. He had sold out the entire world for a few fleeting years of comfort and attachment.

In which case…

"…Shinya has to come back." If Shinya didn't come back to life, Guren had violated the taboo for nothing.

Ferid chuckled. "Such hubris. I love it!"

Guren ignored him, pounding again on Shinya's chest. "Wake up, Shinya."

But Shinya's eyes remained closed.

"I'm begging you, wake up!" he screamed.

But Shinya's eyes remained closed.

If this was a dream, Guren just wanted it to end. For the last ten years his one wish had been to wake up from the nightmare that was his life, but the nightmare never seemed to end. It only got worse.

The vampire reached for Shinya again. Guren was unable to react in time.

Vampires were fast, preternaturally so. And this was no ordinary vampire, it was a noble. A vampire noble's power was on an entirely different plane from that of even ordinary vampires.

Ferid curved his hand into a blade-like claw and thrust it straight into Shinya's chest.

"Bastard!" Guren bellowed, but he was far too late. Ferid had torn a gaping hole in Shinya's chest and his hand now clutched the boy's heart. Ferid squeezed, violently, almost as if he were working an air pump.

He's going to kill him, thought Guren. *Shinya will be lost!*

But of course, Shinya was already dead.

"Stop it!" Guren shouted, when suddenly—

"Gagh," a strangled cough escaped Shinya's lips. Followed by a long rasping wheeze, as his throat gulped down air.

In.

And out.

The sound of Shinya breathing.

"Sh…Shinya?"

"Ooh♪, would you look at that!" Ferid cut in, pumping the hand that held Shinya's heart. He was making it beat, taking the place of Shinya's own pulse. "And now it's beating on its own—aren't I something. Ferid Bathory, the brilliant surgeon!"

Ferid removed his hand, and the color returned to Shinya's pale cheeks. The wound in his chest began to close. His strained, shallow breathing became the steady breath of sleep.

He was alive!

Shinya had come back to life!

But Guren bit his tongue. He wasn't sure if the resurrection was complete, so it was probably safer not to touch Shinya just yet.

Guren had no idea how it all worked, bringing a person back to life. Nor why it was taboo to do so.

But Shinya was back.

He didn't understand the why and how of it, he just knew that Shinya was breathing again—

"Ha..." A broken sigh escaped Guren's lips. "Ha... Ha ha..." Soon he was laughing, his face almost cracking into tears.

Mahiru was dead.

And Guren had violated the taboo. But he had succeeded, he had brought his friends back to life.

The moment he realized this, an incredible weariness washed over him. It had been days since he had last rested, and he suddenly felt it in his very bones.

Hounded at every step, Guren and his friends had been forced to flee the Order of the Imperial Demons, cutting through scores of men before finally arriving at this laboratory.

And when they got there, his friends had been killed.

Mahiru was dead too.

He had lost everything—

Ordinarily, that would have been the end—the end of the tale. Tragically ever after. Guren's friends and family would be dead, with no hope of getting them back; things couldn't get any worse.

But there was more to this story.

"..."

What would Guren reap?

He knew only one thing for sure: He had broken his promise, to Shinya and all his friends. He had broken his promise to stay on the right path, to remain weak even if it meant they all died here. He had violated the taboo.

Guren fell heavily to his knees. He was completely exhausted. All strength seemed to drain from his body, and he chuckled in a colorless voice, "Ha…hahaha…"

The vampire peered down at him, his interest piqued. "What fun you seem to be having."

Guren slumped to the floor, still covered head to toe in blood, and stared up at Ferid.

There were no bloodstains on Ferid's arm. It remained pristine, despite the fact that he had just thrust his hand inside Shinya's chest. The blood in Shinya's chest must have already congealed.

Shinya had died, and then come back to life.

God would never forgive what Guren had done.

The world would never forgive what he had done.

And the vampires, who sought to maintain order in the world, would never forgive what he had done.

"Are you here to kill me?" asked Guren, gazing up at Ferid from where he sat.

Ferid, however, turned his back on Guren and walked toward one of the other coffins.

One coffin among seven.

Not one that belonged to Norito, Mito, Shigure, Sayuri, or Shinya, but which held one of the men Guren didn't know.

"This one looks disgusting," Ferid said, staring down at the stranger. "Not nearly so delicious as the rest of you. Though personally I prefer the blood of children." As he spoke, Ferid dragged the man bodily from the coffin and lifted him up by the neck.

At which the man opened his eyes.

"A… Ahhh! What happened?!" His gaze finally lit on Ferid. "Who are you?! Where am I?!"

"What happened, you ask?" replied Ferid with a twinkle in his eye. "You mean you don't remember the last thing that happened to you?"

"The last... What do you mean?"

"The last thing you remember, your final memory. Do you remember what happened at the end?"

"The...the end...? I can't... I don't remember..." The man tried to think, but he was clearly very confused, which was only natural. He had been dead. Guren had checked, the man's heartbeat and respiration had stopped completely. He had been dead, and now he had come back to life. No wonder he was confused.

Guren stared at him through narrowed eyes.

The man was confused, or perhaps his memory was clouded. Did he have no memory of dying? Or had the shock been so great that his mind had simply suppressed it—?

"Y... Yes, I remember," the man went on. "I was chosen... They told me...if I joined their experiment, they'd pay for my girlfriend's treatment."

Ferid nodded, amused. "So your girlfriend is sick?"

"Yes."

"With what?"

"It's called Elijah's Disease..."

"Never heard of it."

"The doctors say that without treatment she won't live to be thirty. But the disease is so rare that the treatments cost a fortune."

"Hmm... And how old is your girlfriend now?"

"Twenty-two."

"Ah, over thirteen, then. Your girlfriend is already dead, my friend."

"What?! But... They told me if I joined the experiment, they'd pay for her treatments! They said they'd start them right away!" The man began to lose control. He grabbed Ferid by the arm and started screaming, "That wasn't the deal! That wasn't the deal!!"

Who had made a deal with this man?

The Brotherhood of a Thousand Nights?

The Imperial Demons?

Someone else entirely?

It might even have been Mahiru. This had all been her plan, after all. Her plan to escape her own fate.

"You're telling me she's dead?!" the man screamed. "She's already dead?!" He was weeping.

This man probably had some drama of his own—his own life, his own fate. Each of us has our fate, that storm which blows even as we are washed out to sea, lost and unable to see the shore, sweeping us up in its towering waves to hammer home the baffling truth of our own insignificance.

At least, that was the only kind of world Guren had ever known.

"They promised me! They promised me they'd cure her!" the man screamed.

Guren stared at him, feeling for a moment as if it were himself he was looking at.

Ferid grinned wolfishly. "You misunderstand. Elijah's Disease didn't kill your girlfriend. Her cause of death was something else entirely."

The man glared at Ferid, tears streaming down his face. "What did you do to her?!"

"Nothing at all. But he did," said Ferid, turning to look at Guren with his bewitching red eyes. He was still grinning.

The man also turned toward Guren. His eyes were filled with hate.

Guren understood all too well what the man was feeling: he had found a target for his revenge. Everyone needed something to live for in a world like this—a world so full of despair.

"Is it true?" the man asked. "Did you do it?"

Guren didn't answer.

" … "

"Did you do it?!"

" … "

"Answer me! Did you kill my girlfriend?!"

" … "

"I'll kill you."

" … "

"I'll fucking kill you."

" … "

"I swear I'll kill you, no matter what!"

Ferid had asked the man how old his girlfriend was, and pronounced her dead because she was over thirteen.

Mahiru had told Guren something similar.

She'd said that only children would survive. Children and those possessed by demons, and that no normal adult humans could live in this world.

If that was true, and the world outside the laboratory had already met its end, then this man had every right to be angry.

Guren deserved his anger.

He deserved to be killed.

He had brought the world to ruin and laid waste to the future of all humankind, with no concern for anything but his own egotistical desires—he deserved to die.

" … "

Ferid smiled. "Kill him? Yes! An excellent idea! But if you're going to do it, you'd better do it now. I wonder if you have it in you, though. He's very strong, you know. After all, we're talking about a man narcissistic enough to sell the whole world down the river for his own selfish reasons. So whose ego do you think is stronger, his or yours? Go on, let's find out."

Ferid opened his hand and let the man fall to the floor. He immediately scrambled to his feet and pelted towards Guren.

"You're deaaaaaaaad!!"

The man was flailing his fists at Guren, sobbing through his battle cry. Guren made no effort to resist, quietly enduring the man's blows. To his face, his chest, his stomach. The man gouged his thumbs into Guren's eyes, but this too he simply let happen. His eyeballs were squashed like jelly, and he could feel the man's thumbs invading his sockets.

But through it all, Guren felt no pain.

The man was just an ordinary person.

Guren, however, had the demon's curse inside him. He was possessed by a demon, possessed by ruin.

"Die! Die! Die! Die!" the man screamed, punching Guren over and over again in the face where he lay fallen on the ground. But Guren could not die.

The demon's curse regenerated the damage faster than the man could cause it, and Guren's eyes, his skin, his tissue, all of it returned to normal in an instant.

"What are you?! What the hell are youuuu?!"

Guren slowly reached up and took hold of the man's arm.

"Let me go!" the man shouted.

"I'm sorry... I can't let you kill me."

"You think I give a shit?! Give her back to me!"

"I don't know anything about your girlfriend...but there's something I want to ask you."

"Shut up! Shut up! Shut up! I'm gonna kill you..."

"Do you remember dying?" Guren asked.

Guren Ichinose: Resurrection at Nineteen

This was important. He needed to know whether Shinya, Norito, Mito, Shigure, and Sayuri would remember their deaths.

If they did…

"…"

…then all of this despair, the responsibility for violating the taboo—they would have to share that burden with Guren.

That is, if they could even forgive him for what he had done. He had broken his promise. He should never have done what he did.

If they didn't remember, however—

"You were dead," Guren told the man. "Dead. Don't you remember?"

The man's eyes grew wide.

He wore a frightened look, the look of a man staring into some yawning abyss of fear. "What are you saying."

"Do you remember—"

But the man suddenly wrapped his arms around his face and began screaming, "S-Stop it! A-Aieee!" Something was clearly wrong. "It's a lie, you're lying! Why would you…"

A light began to surface in the man's eyes, as if some bright *thing* was devouring him from within, body and soul.

His entire body began to glow.

But it was the glow of sin.

Guren wasn't sure how, but he knew it to be true. *Something* told him it was so. Guren had done that which must never be done. He had disturbed something that should remain untouched. It was sin. Punishment. Taboo. Despair.

That despair began to shine forth from within the man's body, brighter and brighter, tearing at his flesh.

"Aaaiiiiiiiiieeeeeeeeeeeeeeeeeeeeeeeeeeeeeeee!!" His screams grew shrill, and his body began to float above the ground.

Howling.

Cursing.

Despair.

Rancor.

Until finally the man's body exploded in a thunderous burst of light and was gone, vanishing like mist.

"Ngh!" A grunt of surprise escaped Guren's lips.

The man was gone.

Not a shred of him remained.

Erased, as if he had never existed.

"..."

Guren narrowed his eyes. It almost seemed as if—the man had been annihilated by the knowledge that he had already died.

"Well, well..." said Ferid. "Most impressive. Your ego has claimed yet another life. Mahiru was right, the demon's hold on you is strong. Unless perhaps you're a demon yourself at this point?"

"..."

Guren looked at Ferid. The vampire certainly seemed to be enjoying himself.

"There were seven coffins, and you left those strangers in two of them. Why? Because you needed a test case. You intended to use them as test subjects, to make sure your friends' resurrections went smoothly. And so they did. Your planning certainly paid off. It seems your friends won't remember being resurrected. And if they ever find out, they'll be annihilated. And we can't let that happen, now, can we? Good thing you had a guinea pig, wouldn't you say?"

Guren stood up, ignoring all of this. His gouged-out eyes were already completely healed. Ferid was right, Guren thought. He wasn't human anymore.

But that very lack of humanity might be the only reason he was

still alive.

Mahiru had said that raising the dead would invite divine punishment.

A virus would spread, and everyone over the age of thirteen would be wiped out.

But Guren was already sixteen. Old enough, in other words, for the virus to have killed him.

And yet here he stood, alive and well—was it because he had already fused with his demon?

Or, as Ferid had suggested, was he himself completely transformed into a demon at this point?

"..."

Guren turned his gaze on the coffins that held his friends.

Shinya, Norito, Mito, Shigure, and Sayuri remained asleep.

"These guys are smart," Guren said, as he peered down at their sleeping faces. "If they wake up here, they're sure to figure out that they'd been dead."

"Hmm. So what do you propose to do?"

The first man had woken up the moment Ferid removed him from his coffin. The same would probably hold true for Shinya and the others.

In which case...

"I need to get ahold of some anesthetic. Something to make them sleep a little longer."

Guren scanned the room. This was a laboratory, after all. A laboratory for forbidden experiments into raising the dead. Surely they would have plenty of anesthetic.

A quick search paid off.

There were anesthetics, truth serums, temporary poisons. Anything one could imagine, from drugs Guren recognized on sight to substances he couldn't even begin to identify.

He selected an anesthetic and injected his five friends with it. It should keep them from waking up a while longer.

Just to be safe, he waited long enough for the drug to take full effect. The one he had chosen usually knocked a person out in a matter of minutes. Guren waited twenty.

He still couldn't be sure, however. The resurrection effect might override the anesthesia, meaning his friends could still wake up as soon as they were removed from the coffins. Just in case, Guren readied another syringe in his left hand before finally grabbing Shinya by the collar.

His clothes were stained with blood.

It was a mix of their enemies' blood and Shinya's own, and probably even some of Guren's as well.

Guren tightened his grip. "Here we go, Shinya. Don't you dare wake up."

Shinya, for his part, remained asleep. He continued to breathe slowly, his face peaceful.

Guren stared at him a moment longer, and then finally dragged him from the coffin.

"..."

"Shinya?"

"..."

"Shinya? You asleep?"

"..."

"You're asleep, right? You're not going to wake up on me, are you?"

"..."

"Alright."

Guren let out a sigh of relief. He hoisted Shinya over his shoulder, then raised his eyes. What next? How could he bring Shinya and the others back without them realizing they had died?

First things first, he had to take a look outside.

Guren still had no idea what was happening out there.

Had the world ended, as Mahiru had said it would?

Or had it all been a lie, was he just being manipulated by her once again?

Guren looked at the floor between the seven coffins, where the resurrection ritual had been performed. There was a hole, perfectly sized for the katana that had been thrust into it.

The sword was a cursed weapon—Guren's weapon—which held the demon known as Noya. But the last thing Noya had said to Guren, his voice filled with panic, was that Mahiru was absorbing him.

Mahiru had used Noya to stab herself in the chest. And then she had disappeared.

Guren wasn't sure if Mahiru was dead, or if something else had happened to her. Mahiru was always ten steps ahead of Guren. Her actions remained a mystery.

Guren stared at the sword.

Was it Noya, or Mahiru?

Either way, he needed a weapon if he was going to go outside.

The enemy had been on their heels every step of the way to the lab, and they might be waiting outside even now. Guren needed to be ready.

Or the resurrections might have utterly transformed the world outside, it might be more dangerous than ever—all the more reason for Guren to be armed.

Yet he couldn't bring himself to draw the sword from the hole where it stood.

Guren Ichinose: Resurrection at Nineteen

What if it cancelled the resurrection, and Shinya, Norito, Mito, Shigure, and Sayuri died all over again?

"Sorry…" he said, still holding Shinya. "You guys wait here. I'm going to take a look outside."

"…"

Naturally, no one answered him. They were all still sleeping under the effects of the anesthetic.

Guren nodded, satisfied, and began to walk away.

As he did so, a high-pitched, metallic scraping sound pierced the air.

Guren's sword was spinning through the air. It flew across the room and slid itself into the sheath at Guren's waist.

"…"

Guren glanced down at the sheath.

At the sword girded at his waist.

"Noya…?" he ventured.

"…"

There was no answer.

"Mahiru?"

"…"

Still no answer.

But he could sense that the sword had changed. He and Noya had been deeply intertwined, and he knew right away that the sword at his waist was something else.

What that was, however, was a question which would have to wait. Right now Guren had other things to worry about. His first concern was to make sure Shinya and the others were safe.

Guren started walking.

Ferid followed along behind him. "Taking a little stroll outside?"

"Yeah."

"Exciting, isn't it? Who knows what's happened out there."

"Don't you?"

"Only rumors. Of what would happen if a resurrection was ever performed."

"What kind of rumors?"

"Nothing you haven't heard."

In other words, apocalypse.

Only demons and children left alive.

Guren trudged down the long, long corridor to the lab and boarded a series of elevators leading to the surface, Shinya still slung over his shoulder.

Ferid joined him. He seemed to be thoroughly enjoying the whole situation.

On their way to the surface they didn't encounter a single living soul. Everyone was dead. But that didn't mean a virus had killed them. In fact it seemed unlikely, since Guren and the others had killed essentially everyone who blocked their path to the ceremonial hall below.

And besides, all the people here would have been equipped with cursed swords. They must have died at the hands of Guren and his companions, then.

"You're a veritable mass murderer," Ferid said as they boarded the third elevator.

"That's rich, coming from a bloodsucking vampire," Guren shot back.

"We don't actually kill very often. We only take the blood we need."

"Yeah, well."

Guren Ichinose: Resurrection at Nineteen

"That's all you've got to say? Try and show a little interest."

At this, Guren turned to face Ferid. "Why haven't you killed me? I thought the vampires wanted to stop the human race from violating the taboo."

"Yes, that's true."

"So why aren't you doing your job?"

"I have a terrible work ethic."

"If the world really has come to an end, you're just as—"

"Would it make you feel better if I were also to blame?" Ferid cut in. "Ha! Fine, we'll split the sin right down the middle. How does that suit you?"

"..."

"Alright then, I'll play the bad guy if you like. I'm used to the role, and if it makes this all easier for you to bear, so much the better."

"..."

"But just so we're on the same page, what I said earlier is true: we vampires don't kill often. We have no urge to. In fact, we can't maintain much in the way of desire at all. We have our thirst for blood and the despair that comes from this interminable life, and little else."

"..."

"So we rarely kill. Even killing feels meaningless to us. Either that or we kill a great deal, since it feels meaningless either way. Those vampires, the great killers, are broken inside. Now then, which do you suppose I am? I'm sure it's a very meaningful question for someone in your predicament. After all, you're not broken, so it would bring you no comfort to share your sin with someone who is. What good would it do to share the blame with a madman? So which do you think I am? Go on, guess!"

Ferid certainly liked to talk.

Guren studied the vampire. "I really don't care," he said finally. After all, he was clearly the latter.

Ferid's eyes were very intelligent. Behind those puckish eyes, Guren could detect intellect and reason terrifying in their intensity, and behind that, madness. But behind the madness lay reason once more.

Guren stared into Ferid's twinkling eyes for a long moment before he spoke again. "Fine. Which one are you?"

"Go on, guess."

"How should I know?"

"Hahaha, to be honest, even I don't know. But dear old mama used to say—"

"Mama?"

"Yes. The woman who bore me from her loins. She was very beautiful."

"Fine, what did your mama say about you?"

Ferid grinned impishly, and replied, "Here is what she said." He spread his arms wide as if he were standing on a stage. *"What have you done. Why are you doing this. It's horrible. So horrible."*

"…"

"It's all too horrible. No, Ferid, please. Don't kill me. Pleaaaseaaghhhh."

"…That's not funny."

"No, it's not, is it. Mother certainly didn't think so, anyway, not after she was dead."

"…"

"Heh…heheh…hahahahaha!" Ferid began to cackle, there in the elevator, apparently amused with himself.

Guren had no idea if the story was just a joke, or if it was true.

Guren Ichinose: Resurrection at Nineteen

The only thing he knew for sure was that he was in the presence of madness.

Or was it intelligence?

Whatever it was, Guren had encountered it before. He had been struck with the same feeling when speaking with Mahiru: a bottomless terror he could never plumb, no matter how he tried.

Although, it had felt as if Mahiru retained a bit more of her reason than Ferid seemed to—

"There is one thing I want to ask," said Guren. Something about this vampire had piqued his interest after all. Namely, whether or not he had been colluding with Mahiru. And if so, what the mad pair could possibly have talked about.

"And what is that, Guren Ichinose?" inquired Ferid, turning to look at him.

"Were you in contact with Mahiru?"

Ferid grinned in response. "Oh, yes. Every kind of contact."

"!"

"Kidding."

"!!"

"Not kidding."

"?!!"

"Really, I'm only kidding~"

This was hopeless. It was impossible to get a straight answer out of this—

Ferid lunged suddenly. In the tight confines of the elevator, he grabbed Guren by the neck and slammed him against the wall—

"Grk!" Guren could only manage a grunt.

Ferid's face drew near, his pupils dilated amid the crimson of his eyes.

He opened his mouth wide, exposing the razor-sharp fangs

within. "Your blood seems so much sweeter than Mahiru's, you see."

"..."

Dammit—Guren's mouth moved, but nothing came out. With his free hand, the one not holding Shinya, he grabbed Ferid's hair from behind, desperately trying to pull him away. It was like trying to move a brick wall.

The difference in their strength was so great that Guren was like an infant in the hands of a full-grown man. Despair washed over him.

"Urk..."

Ferid, meanwhile, seemed as amused as ever. "I'm telling you I want to drink your blood, and I could do it so easily if I wished. I'm so much stronger than you."

"..."

"But where would be the fun in that? So tedious. I want you to want me to drink your blood, to want it from the bottom of your heart. It's so much more interesting that way."

"..."

"Strange, isn't it? That a vampire should desire something like that."

"Urkrk, urkrkrk, urkrkrkrk."

Ferid's face was a hair's breadth from Guren's as he spoke, his hand wrapped around Guren's windpipe.

The vampire's face was eerily beautiful, his skin a flawless alabaster mask. But it didn't seem beautiful to Guren. All he felt was fear. Fear of the madman there before him.

Of this noble vampire who had lost his mind.

"Here, let me offer you a proposal," said Ferid. "How about I drain the blood from your precious friend first?"

"?!"

"And then I'll kill him. Wouldn't that be something? Imagine it, you've betrayed the entire world, moved heaven and earth to bring your friend back to life, only for me to come along and suck him dry."

"Urk, rk." Guren clenched his fist once more. He began summoning the curse into his free arm.

The demon's power flowed through his body.

Power. Give me power.

Guren had to act quickly. If he didn't kill the vampire now, the consequences would be dire.

He didn't care if it was Noya or Mahiru inside the sword, just so long as whoever it was gave him enough power to kill Ferid—

All of a sudden, Ferid punched him full force in the face.

"Gah!"

Ferid punched him again, this time in the stomach, and Guren felt his organs rupture. Blood geysered from his mouth.

"Whoopsie-daisy!" exclaimed Ferid, taking a step back to avoid being soiled by Guren's blood.

Guren couldn't move. He felt paralyzed. His knees buckled, and he collapsed to the floor.

"Dear oh dear," murmured Ferid, waving the hand he had just used to punch Guren. "That's not enough to kill you, though. Trust me, I know of what I speak. I've had plenty of practice ripping apart demon-possessed humans in the course of my interrogations."

"..."

"Your organs can burst, and you'll still heal. It's revolting. Humans are supposed to be so fragile, it's what makes them beautiful."

The vampire reached down and picked up Shinya's still-sleeping form.

Dammit. Dammit! Guren was helpless to stop him.

Ferid opened his mouth wide, and—

"Leave him alone." Guren's organs had begun to heal and he finally managed to speak, just as Ferid's mouth was about to clamp down on Shinya's exposed neck.

Ferid paused and glared down at Guren, his cold red eyes just visible above the neck of his prey.

"Yes…?" he prompted, seeming pleased.

"Leave him alone," repeated Guren.

"Sorry, what was that? Did you say, 'Please leave him alone, o my lord and master'?"

"If I say it…will you leave him be?"

"A fine question. Honestly, I'd rather you put your own spin on it. But think about it for a moment. Have you forgotten who got little Shinya Hiragi's heart to beat again? I'm sure you're very proud of yourself for all the effort you put in to try and resurrect him, but, what's this? In the end I believe you owe it all to the brilliant surgeon extraordinaire! I'm still waiting for you to express your gratitude."

"…I'm very grateful."

"Then *show* me how grateful you really are."

Guren looked over at his friend. Past Shinya's face, he could see the elevator display moving steadily closer to the ground floor. They would reach the surface before long.

Right now they were still underground, but soon they would emerge to stand beneath the sun's rays.

And Guren had to somehow keep his friends alive long enough to make their way back to the world above.

In which case—

"Fine," Guren said. "You win."

He reached up and loosened the collar of his combat uniform, exposing his neck.

Guren Ichinose: Resurrection at Nineteen

Ferid swallowed expectantly, betraying for the first time some glimmer of desire.

"Hurry up and drink," Guren told him.

Ferid laughed. "Is that really your idea of supplication?"

"You said you wanted me to put my own spin on it."

"Ha! L'enfant terrible!" The vampire set Shinya down. He stepped closer, and lifted Guren off the ground, gripping him by the hair and exposing his neck. "Now you can truly say you saved little Shinya Hiragi. I was serious about killing him, you know."

"You'll just have to settle for my blood."

"Such bluster! Fine, we can play this game." Ferid opened his mouth. His fangs pierced Guren's throat, and he began to slurp away at Guren's blood.

The pleasure Guren felt was indescribable.

He already knew how it would feel, though; Mahiru had drunk his blood as well. As a person's blood is drained away and they race towards death, the brain releases a flood of endorphins.

Guren stared absently at the elevator ceiling as Ferid drank—it gave him something to focus on, to avoid drowning in that rush of pleasure.

The floor display read:

B7.

B6.

B5.

Ferid drank, and drank.

B4.

B3.

B2.

Slurp, slurp, sluuuuurp.

B1.

They arrived at the surface.

"Ground floor, everybody off!" exclaimed Ferid, removing his lips from Guren's neck as if he had been watching the display the whole time. "Delectable. I can almost taste the sin. Now then, let's see how things are out there." He tossed Guren to the floor.

Having lost so much blood, Guren couldn't summon the strength to stand.

The demon's curse—if he could just rely on its power, in place of his own blood...

"..."

His mind felt fuzzy, and he was having trouble focusing his eyes. But he was aware of the elevator doors slowly beginning to open. Unless he was mistaken, the elevator should let out onto the streets of Shinjuku. That was where the laboratory was located, anyway.

If a virus really had spread and killed every single adult, the sight that awaited them would be a grim one indeed.

The doors opened, and light flooded the elevator.

Ferid turned and looked out.

"What do you see," Guren asked the vampire. "How is it out there?"

"Hm? It's marvelous."

"What...do you mean?"

"Whoops, I'm afraid we've got company. You might not survive this one. Unless I protect you, of course."

"Company? Who could—"

"There's no time to think. They're nearly here. If you want me to protect you, you'll have to ask. Tell me you want to make a bargain."

"What do you mean, bargain?"

"Enough! Ask me. Beg me. Do that, and I will guide you through this ruined world," pronounced Ferid, placing his hand on the sword at his waist.

Ruined.

Ferid had called it a ruined world.

Had the virus really spread?

Were the adults all dead, the world turned upside down?

It was all Guren's fault.

Guren, and his selfish ego.

Just then, a voice from outside interrupted his musings. It was a woman's voice. Beautiful.

But if all the adults were dead, whose could it be?

"Ferid Bathory," the voice said. "Explain yourself."

"Siren! Fancy meeting you here."

"Don't give me that. This was your assigned territory. And yet I'm told you did not arrive in time to stop the experiment. So why are you here now?"

In response, Ferid drew the sword at his waist and took a step forward. "This is all a big misunderstanding. I only just arrived myself, I'm as shocked as you are…"

"Stay back! Why do you draw your sword?"

"I'm telling you, this is all a misunderstanding."

"I am of the sixth rank. You cannot simply—"

"Kyahahahahahahahahahhahahahahahaha!!"

Ferid hurtled out of the elevator.

"What's this? All of you, battle formation! Seventh Rank Progenitor Ferid Bathory has betrayed us… Shit, my arm… Die, you bastaaaaaaaaaaaaard!"

Guren heard a cacophony of clashing swords.

Several minutes passed, but Guren still hadn't recovered enough to stand. His internal organs had been pulverized. He was low on blood. And hell, he was starving. At this point, his body was running on fumes.

But he couldn't give up now. It was too late in the game to wash his hands of responsibility and let himself die.

As he sat helplessly on the floor, he looked toward Shinya, who lay sleeping beside him. "Hahaha, this is some mess we've gotten ourselves into, isn't it, Shinya?"

But his friend merely continued to sleep peacefully.

"Tsk. Can't believe you're sleeping at a time like this."

"…"

"I guess shit outside this elevator is pretty crazy. Seems as though the world has ended. Everyone's probably dead."

"…"

"It's my fault."

"…"

"I'm sorry. I…"

"…"

"I just wanted a little more time with you and the others. Is that so wrong?"

"…"

"Is it?"

"…"

"Maybe it is, at that. But what's done is done. Think you can ever forgive me?"

But how could Guren possibly hope to be forgiven? If the world outside had been destroyed, then what Ferid said was true: Guren really was a mass murderer. The worst, most despicable killer in history.

How could he ever atone for a sin so great?

Guren's internal organs had finally healed enough for him to move. "Unh… Still low on blood, though…" he murmured, struggling to his feet.

Outside the elevator, the sounds of swordplay had ceased. He didn't need to see to know that the battle was over, he could sense it.

"I'm gonna take a look outside," he said to Shinya, pressing the HOLD button. "You wait here."

Guren stepped outside.

This elevator was an emergency escape route, different from the way they had come. As such, it opened directly onto the surface. He wasn't sure what street he was on, only that it was a sidewalk close to a subway entrance.

There was no sign of Ferid or the vampires he had been fighting.

A deathly silent world spread out before him, mountains of corpses filling the landscape as far as the eye could see. Countless bodies were piled near the subway station, practically blocking the entrance. There was no path that was free of bodies, no hope of avoiding them.

The people had all died clutching at their chests or necks, their faces contorted in pain. There were so many corpses. They were literally beyond counting.

"…huff…huff…"

Crashed and overturned cars were everywhere. Tendrils of flame rose all around the city, and the sounds of explosions could be heard echoing through the streets, again and again and again. But there were no human voices. No screams.

Death.

It was a city of death.

Everyone was dead.

"…huff…huff…huff…"

Guren stared out at the destruction.

At the despair.

His breathing grew rapid, his pulse raced.

The end, it was really the end.

Everyone was dead.

And he was the one who had killed them.

He stared at the corpses piled high all around him.

It was probably the same all over the world.

Wait, what about what Mahiru had said?

"Children… I thought the children were supposed to survive?" Guren scanned his surroundings, but he didn't see a single living soul. He realized that none of the bodies belonged to children either, however. Of course, he was in the business district of Shinjuku, so there might not have been any children to begin with.

"…huff…huff…huff…" The overwhelming sense of despair made Guren feel sick. He clutched at his chest. How was he supposed to go on living in a world like this? "Why did I survive? What was the point…" he began to say, but he bit his tongue. He turned around. Shinya was still asleep on the floor of the elevator.

His family was alive, and sleeping.

"…"

Guren felt his eyes grow wet, and was aware of tears spilling down his cheeks.

But what good would crying do? Crying wasn't going to save anyone. Was God looking down on him now, did God see his tears? These crocodile tears he now wept, too little, too late.

Guren turned his misty eyes toward the sky. It was clear, not a single cloud to be seen. It was sickening how beautiful that nighttime sky was.

"Dammit… What am I supposed to do now?"

There was no answer.

He wiped away his tears with his blood-soaked sleeve. He had no right to cry.

He was the one who had chosen all of this.

He had brought them back.

He had violated the taboo.

And the world had ended.

It had been his choice. He had known that this would happen, and he had done it anyway. He had no one to blame but himself. It was all his fault.

"…"

And if he ever told anyone what he had done, if Shinya and the others ever found out, they might disappear again, forever.

So he could never speak of it again.

He could never complain.

Could never ask for advice.

Could never even appear troubled.

When Shinya, Norito, Mito, Shigure, and Sayuri got their first glimpse of this new world, Guren would have to look just as surprised as they were. He would have to act hopeless, get angry, try to blame someone else for what had happened.

Otherwise, Shinya and the others might realize the truth. That he was the one who was responsible for it all, who had brought back the dead.

So Guren could never again wrestle with his guilt. He could never again cry over what he had done.

This would have to be the last time.

"Uf, uf, uf."

This was the last time he would ever have the privilege of crying.

"WAAAAAAAAAAAAAAAAAAAAAAAAAAAAAAAAAAAAAAAAA!"

He howled, beating his fists against the earth, choking on his own despair.

His cries echoed across the beautiful night sky. But there was no one left to hear him.

Everyone was dead.

And Guren had killed them.

"..."

Guren cried until his throat was ragged, then got back to his feet. His tears had already dried, but he scrubbed his cheeks over and over again to make sure no evidence was left.

He drew a deep breath.

Let it out.

He was calm now.

Ready to shoulder the burden of his guilt.

He thrust out his chin, returned to the elevator, and hoisted his friend back onto his shoulder. "Shinya, it's time to live."

But now we wind the clock back even further.

To a few minutes before the end of the world.

Christmas night, 8:24 p.m.

On the outskirts of a town, one of several in Aichi Prefecture home to large contingents of adherents to the religious syndicate known as the Order of the Imperial Moon, deep in a forest reserve, off-limits to trespassers, stood a small mountain.

There among the trees, some hours' hike up paths hardly worthy of the name, stood a lone torii. One would assume it had been placed there in honor of some god, but in truth no god was enshrined here.

Indeed, the entire reserve belonged to the Narumi Clan, one of the Imperial Moon's largest and most fervent followers. And the Imperial Moon did not hold with gods in the first place, so it was only natural that none would be enshrined on their land.

But in that case, why was there a torii there at all—?

"…"

Makoto Narumi couldn't figure it out.

He had blasphemously strung the torii with lights, and was using the area to train—but he couldn't help thinking, if there was no god, then why was there a torii here in the first place?

The question had never occurred to Makoto before. He had been coming here ever since he was little, but the presence of the torii was a mystery to him.

Makoto narrowed his eyes in thought.

His hair had a brownish tint to it, and he sported a mole beneath one of his sloping eyes. Although he was only eleven, his body was lean and taut from training. Ever since he was a baby he had been told that one day he would join the inner circle of the Order of the Imperial Moon.

A wooden sword hung at his waist.

As usual, he had spent the whole day training in magic and swordcraft, but midway through he had knocked off and come to this mountain.

Makoto sat perched amid the branches of a great cedar tree, at the very top of the mountain; the tree was so tall it seemed to afford a view of the entire town. From this vantage he gazed down at the vermilion torii.

"Hey, Shusaku," he began. "Why do you suppose this torii is on my family's land?"

To which the calm, black-haired boy seated on a slightly lower branch replied, "Shouldn't you be more worried about heading back, Makoto? We're going to get in trouble."

"We're not going to get in trouble."

"*I'm* going to get in trouble."

"No one cares if *you* get in trouble."

"That's not very nice, Makoto." But the other boy sounded as unruffled as ever.

His name was Shusaku Iwasaki and he was eleven, just like Makoto.

According to their parents, Shusaku was Makoto's prospective retainer, destined to serve him in the future. But Makoto had never thought of Shusaku that way.

He and Shusaku had been raised side by side—they had played together, trained together—for as long as Makoto could remember. Shusaku was like a brother to him, or at least his oldest friend.

One day when the boys were six, Shusaku suddenly began to show deference toward Makoto and speak formally when addressing him. Makoto was so pissed off that they got into a fight. Shusaku had always called him Mako, but all of a sudden he was calling him "Lord Makoto." He said he had to, that it was just the way things were—so Makoto punched him in the face.

—That's bullshit, take it back! You and me, we're brothers!

Shusaku insisted, however. He said it was better this way, for both of them. That it was what the future had in store.

But Makoto refused to accept it. He decided that as long as Shusaku continued to call him "Lord," he wouldn't speak a word to him.

Once Makoto made up his mind about something, he was adamant. A leader could never waver—that was the Narumi way. He had to be strong. Days passed as Makoto stubbornly refused to utter a single word to his friend.

Shusaku continued to follow him around like a puppy the entire time, the expression on his face as placid as ever. Doggedly, he tried again and again to get Makoto to speak to him. The two were never apart, so the situation was probably just as hard on Shusaku.

Lord Makoto, please talk to me.

Lord Makoto, I'll be scolded if things keep on this way.

Lord Makoto. Lord Makoto. Lord Makoto.

Three months of silence passed after Shusaku began addressing

Guren Ichinose: Resurrection at Nineteen

Makoto as "Lord," until one day Shusaku finally gave in.

That day too, they had been sitting in the cedar tree atop the mountain.

—Fine. I won't call you lord anymore. And I'll speak normally. But not in front of the grownups! And I can't call you Mako anymore, either. I'll call you Makoto from now on. Deal?

Makoto smiled the smile he had been holding back for the past three months.

—I still like Mako better.

—You've gotta meet me halfway here.

—Seriously though, three months? I can't believe you're so stubborn.

—You're the stubborn one! I cried every single night, you know.

—There, there.

From that day forth, Shusaku began calling him Makoto. Which was probably for the best. They would be adults before long, and Makoto sounded more mature than Mako.

They may have only been eleven, but the boys were eager to grow up. They were going to help the Ichinose Clan lead the Order of the Imperial Moon. They were going to change the world!

That meant getting out from under the harsh thumb of the Hiragi Clan, so that the Imperial Moon could claim its rightful glory. Lord Guren was in Tokyo at this very moment, by himself, struggling with all his might to realize that dream.

Makoto and Shusaku had to keep studying and training until they were finally old enough to help Guren. There was no time to waste.

Which is why they had spent the past few days secluding themselves on this mountain. They were learning new magics, and practicing their swordcraft late into the night.

At his father Lord Sakae Ichinose's funeral, Lord Guren had enjoined Makoto to follow him. That was why Makoto was training so hard: because he knew Guren was still fighting to change the world. And Makoto wanted to do his own part to make sure Guren's ambitions were realized.

Since that day he had stepped up his training regimen even further. Naturally, Shusaku had joined him. If they were going to support the Ichinose Clan together, like brothers, they had to grow stronger together, like brothers.

Which is why Makoto brought Shusaku along with him when he ran off to the wilderness. For the past several days, their training had been so fierce that one false move could have spelled death. And now—

"Isn't a torii supposed to enshrine a god?"

Shusaku rolled his eyes in exasperation. "Makoto."

"Yeah?"

"Do you remember what I was doing when you came to get me?"

"How many days ago was that?"

"Five."

"I don't know, what were you doing?"

"I was eating dinner."

"Oh yeah, that's right. You were having croquettes."

"Croquettes are my favorite. But I only got to eat two bites before you dragged me off to the mountains."

"Uh huh."

"We haven't been home in five days."

"Think we've gotten any stronger?"

"We have to go back. I have a schedule, and so do you—"

"I'll never be able to help Lord Guren with the regimen they've got me on," Makoto cut in. "We need to train harder."

"Then tell your instructor…"

"I already did. He said they're going to change the curriculum, but we can't just sit around idly while they do. We need to keep training!"

"I know. But I was having croquettes."

"Wait, are you angry? Relax, I'll buy you come croquettes from the convenience store on our way home."

"But I like my mother's croquettes. You know that."

"Mama's boy."

"What's wrong with that? I'm only eleven," Shusaku shot back. "I barely ever get to see my mother anyway."

Shusaku's mother, Shien Iwasaki, was a famous sorceress. As a celebrity in magical circles, she was constantly traveling the country.

As a result, she was rarely home. As far as Makoto could tell, she hadn't been very involved in Shusaku's day-to-day upbringing. The only thing she could even cook were croquettes, which was why Shusaku made such a big fuss about them. Makoto had eaten them before. They weren't particularly good. The croquettes the servants at home made were way better.

In other words, Shusaku was just a mama's boy.

"Wait a second, is Shien leaving again today?" guessed Makoto.

Shusaku shrugged. "She said she'd only be gone for five days."

"And you want to see your mommy?"

"Uh huh."

Total mama's boy. Makoto nodded. "Fine then. Let's head back."

"You mean it?"

"I want to see Shien, too. She's waaay better at magic than my instructor. Wait, that gives me an idea! We should get Shien to put together a curriculum for us, one that'll help us get stronger all at once!"

"Mom always says the fundamentals are the most important in the end," replied Shusaku.

"Easy for you to say! I bet you're only better than me at magic because you learned it straight from Shien. Cheater."

Or maybe it was just genetics.

Ever since he was little, Shusaku had had a natural talent for magic. If they had spent the same amount of time training, Shusaku's magic would probably have outclassed Makoto's. But because Makoto knew Shusaku had more talent, he had worked twice as hard. He still wasn't sure he had caught up, though.

"I think you're better at magic than I am, Makoto."

"That's because I worked twice as hard."

"You deserve a gold star."

"Hey, are you making fun of me?"

"Pleaaase, can we just go home now?"

Makoto smiled and extended his arm, raising two fingers into the air. He began focusing on the flow of energy through his body that was necessary for performing magic.

"..."

"Before we go," began Makoto, glancing down once more through the branches at the torii, "you still have to answer my question."

"You mean your silly question about the gods?" replied Shusaku, following Makoto's gaze.

"That's the one."

"There are no gods."

"I mean, sure, that's what we were taught." According to the teachings of the Order of the Imperial Moon, there was no greater object of reverence than the Ichinose Clan. "But in that case, what's that torii doing there?"

"Hrm. I never thought about it before, but it is strange. A shrine is supposed to enshrine a god. Plus it's a whole other religion—why would they allow it here? I wonder if there's some connection."

"Maybe we should ask Shien."

"Or maybe if you studied the history of magic—"

"Nah, I bailed on that part of the curriculum. History won't help me get any stronger."

"But at the end of the day it's on your land. It seems like that kind of stuff would be important for a leader to know. It's followers like me who should be skipping magical social studies to focus on getting stronger."

"Lord Guren is the leader. I just want to help him."

"I'm pretty sure Lord Guren would say that knowledge and intelligence are also important."

"Hmm… You're probably right. But while I'm off reading books you'll wind up getting stronger than me," said Makoto.

Shusaku grinned. "That's what I'm here for. You're the fearless leader, I'm just your shield."

"No reason shields shouldn't be smart too, is there?"

"'Spose not…"

"So you hit the books too, shield!"

"You just don't want to have to study on your own."

"Hahaha."

"Anyway, let's go home already, Makoto."

"Okay."

The two were just about to leave,

when suddenly—

It happened.

Something was amiss. An ominous rumbling noise coming from the sky, steadily growing louder.

"Huh? What is that?" Looking up, Makoto quickly spotted the source of the sound.

It was a jumbo jet.

It pierced the clouds, tearing through the darkness, descending at a clearly unnatural angle with its nose tipped toward the ground.

Makoto's eyes grew wide. "Sh-Shit, that can't be right."

By the time the words had left his mouth, the roar of the plane had become deafening.

There were no airports nearby—no reason a passenger plane should be anywhere near there.

It could only mean one thing: the plane was about to crash. And it was headed straight for the town.

"Shusaku! That plane is gonna crash!" Makoto shouted. When he turned toward his friend, however, he spotted three more planes tumbling from the sky.

They were all dropping at a precipitous angle, tracing downward parabolas like shooting stars in a children's book. From where they sat, it looked as if the planes were moving across the sky slowly, but in reality they were hurtling toward the ground with incredible speed—

BOOM BOOM BOOM BOOM BOOM BOOM BOOM

Explosions rang out all around them, coming from every conceivable direction.

Tongues of flame rose on the horizon—the town was burning.

They had only seen four planes go down with their own eyes,

but heard many other explosions in the distance. Of course, there was no way of knowing whether all of them were the sounds of planes crashing, or if there were other explosions mixed in as well.

"What the hell is happening?!" Makoto shouted, but Shusaku didn't know any better than he did.

"Makoto, let's get down from here. We have to get back," said Shusaku, leaping up to the same branch as Makoto and grabbing him by the arm.

Makoto ignored him, turning instead toward the town.

Flames licked the sky, and the explosions continued. The fire was spreading.

Red. Bright red.

A light bright as the morning sun rose from the town and bathed the sky with crimson.

"Is it a terrorist attack? Or war?" Makoto wondered aloud.

Shusaku tugged harder at his arm. "Either way, we have to get out of this tree and turn off the lights on the torii. Whatever's happening, now's not a good time to draw attention to ourselves."

He was right.

Makoto nodded, and leapt down from the branch. He landed on the torii and reached for the lights. "I'm turning them off."

"Do it," said Shusaku, closing his eyes. Makoto followed suit. Closing their eyes would help them adjust to the ensuing darkness. They were in the wilderness, at night. If they turned off the lights just like that, they wouldn't be able to see.

Luckily the sky was clear. There weren't many clouds, and the moon was large and bright. Even without the lights—

Makoto's thoughts were interrupted by another rumble.

Another jet, dropping out of the sky. This one sounded like it was going to hit close by.

"Shit," cursed Makoto, glancing up.

"Hurry," Shusaku urged him.

Makoto closed his eyes.

Turned off the lights.

Opened them again.

But the light from the approaching plane left the area just as bright as before.

"This is crazy!" Makoto yanked the lights free and jumped down from the torii. He threw on the knapsack that held his training gear, and pulled his cell phone out of it. There was no service. "What about yours, Shusaku?"

Shusaku shook his head. His phone didn't have reception either. He threw his own knapsack over his shoulder.

"You ready, Shusaku?"

"I'm ready, Makoto."

The two nodded, and began to run.

They made their way down the dark mountainside at a speed unbelievable for two eleven-year-old boys. Even at top speed, however, they knew it would take a full half hour to reach the bottom.

"There could be trouble waiting..." said Shusaku after a time.

"I know," replied Makoto.

They didn't know what they would be getting into, so they needed to conserve their strength.

The boys slowed down. At this pace, it would probably take them about forty-five minutes to reach the bottom.

Makoto wanted to get down there as soon as possible and find out what was going on, but it was obvious that whatever was happening was well out of the ordinary.

All the more reason to keep a cool head.

Guren Ichinose: Resurrection at Nineteen

A magic-user in the Order of the Imperial Moon always had to stay calm.

Like Lord Guren.

Even when Guren Ichinose's own father had been beheaded before his very eyes, even when video of the event was broadcast worldwide and he was made a laughingstock—Lord Guren had kept his cool.

Makoto pictured it now. If it had been him in Lord Guren's place, would he have been able to keep calm? The answer was a resounding no.

Makoto's father had earned the faith of the Ichinose Clan, and was one of their most capable followers. Makoto loved and respected the man. He wanted to be just like him. And he wanted Lord Guren to rely on him the way Lord Sakae had relied on his father.

Which is why Makoto knew he would have lost his mind if they had done to his father what they had done to Sakae Ichinose.

But Lord Guren had kept it together.

At first Makoto had been angry that he could just stand by passively in the face of all that had been done to him. But now…now Makoto wanted to become just like Lord Guren.

"Keep your cool. Keep your cool. Just like Lord Guren…" Makoto muttered to himself as they descended the mountain.

They reached the bottom exactly forty-five minutes later.

By this point the flurry of crashing jets had ended. There were no more explosions.

A park awaited them at the foot of the mountain, quiet in the night.

There was a clock in the park with a light attached. It read 9:26 p.m.

Beneath the clock was a public restroom. But there was no sign of anyone about.

Not many people visited the park to begin with, though, and its gates were locked at 8:00 p.m. every night.

Rather than head toward the gate, the two boys made a beeline in the direction of their homes. Whenever they came to the park, they just hopped the fence anyway.

They raced by a baseball field, followed by a playground with a slide and sandbox. When they reached the fence they jumped onto it without slowing down, and began to climb over.

A road awaited them on the other side. This, too, was rarely used, but—

" . . . "

Makoto froze, still perched atop the fence. From there he could see an overturned car in the middle of the road.

"What the hell...?"

"An accident?" asked Shusaku, but Makoto shook his head.

"I don't think anybody driving on this road would be going fast enough to flip their car."

They climbed down the fence and walked out into the road. Makoto peered through the windshield of the overturned car. The driver was dead, covered in blood. Half the person's head was gone, caved in where it had smashed into the steering wheel. Makoto couldn't even tell if it was a man or woman. Probably elderly either way.

" . . . "

Makoto lifted his head and looked down the road. Another car had crashed into the wall farther down, where the road curved.

Cars crashed and overturned?

Planes falling from the sky?

Guren Ichinose: Resurrection at Nineteen

"…"

Makoto pressed his hand against his chest as he stared at the wreckage.

Stay cool. Stay cool.

Should they take a look inside the second car, or ignore it and head home?

Shusaku spoke, interrupting his thoughts. "Let's head home."

He was right. Their first order of business was getting back. Makoto had no idea what was going on, but looking inside the other car wasn't going to bring them any answers.

Right now, they needed to get home.

Makoto's father would be waiting for them there, along with his most capable men. Shusaku's mother, the famous sorceress Shien, would almost certainly be there too. If anyone knew what was going on, surely it would be them.

"Alright, let's go," said Makoto.

The two began running, but barely made it a few feet before they stopped again.

As soon as they reached the main road they were confronted with a sea of cars, all of them crashed, or overturned, or burning where their fuel tanks had exploded.

But despite the carnage, it was all eerily quiet. There were no sirens, no police cars or ambulances. This was a disastrous pile-up, but there was no clamor, no tumult.

Everyone inside the cars was dead.

The pedestrians who had been walking on the sidewalk were dead.

"What the hell…? What happened here?"

It looked as if the people had died in pain, clutching at their chests and necks. The bodies on the sidewalk had blood coming out of their mouths and noses.

"Don't touch anyone…" said Shusaku.

He didn't have to tell Makoto, twice.

"Do you think it was some kind of terrorist attack? Like a biological weapon or something?" asked Makoto, still at a loss.

Shusaku shook his head. "I don't know."

"But how come we're still alive?"

"Maybe because we were up on the mountain?"

"We're not up on the mountain now. It looks like it was airborne, whatever it was. And it seems like everyone died all at once." The pedestrians, the people in the cars—it really did look as if they had all died simultaneously. "Maybe it's not contagious anymore? In which case, we're… How do you feel, Shusaku?"

"Me? How do you feel?"

"Healthy as a horse."

"Then maybe it's safe at this point."

"Yeah, maybe… If it is still contagious, we're already screwed. But just to be on the safe side, let's not touch any of the bodies. Might still be dangerous."

The two moved on, threading their way through the bodies.

They came to a house, and Makoto used his wooden training sword to break a window and peek inside. An old couple had died in their living room, huddled around the heater as they watched TV.

Static scratched noisily across the screen. Makoto and Shusaku looked at the television, and then at each other.

According to the clock in the couple's living room, it was 9:45. Prime time. But the television broadcast was down.

What could it mean?

"…"

Were the deaths not confined to their town? Was everyone in

Guren Ichinose: Resurrection at Nineteen

Aichi Prefecture dead? Everyone in Japan? Or could it be that everyone in the entire world was dead?

They had yet to encounter a single living soul since they came down off the mountain.

What the hell did it all mean?

A chill ran down Makoto's spine. What if he and Shusaku were the last two people left alive in the whole world? Once he'd thought it, he—

Surely the same thought had occurred to Shusaku. But he had kept it to himself, so Makoto decided not to say it out loud either.

Makoto just wanted to get home. To see his father. He wanted to run there, as fast as he could. *No, stay cool,* he murmured to himself. *Keep your cool, just like Lord Guren.*

Finally he calmed down enough to say, "We should do some reconnaissance, first."

"How do we go about that?" asked Shusaku.

"We go to a convenience store."

Shusaku nodded enthusiastically. "Of course! We can check the surveillance cameras and see what happened when the planes went down. Makoto, you're a genius!"

"Tell me something I don't know!" Makoto tried to lighten the mood, but he couldn't quite manage a smile.

It didn't take them long to find a convenience store. There were seven people inside: two by the magazine racks, one in the instant noodle aisle, two in front of the bento boxes, and two employees.

They were all dead. Blood trailed from their mouths and noses.

It was like a slaughterhouse.

They climbed over the counter and went into the staff room in back. There they found the body of a person who seemed to have been the manager. They looked around until they found a drawer that fit the keys he was carrying. Inside were a bunch of binders explaining work protocols, among which they found a password and instructions on how to view the surveillance tapes.

Makoto accidentally touched the manager while he was searching him, even got the man's blood on him. But nothing happened. Apparently the disease wasn't transmitted by touch. Though they still couldn't say for sure.

Since he had already touched the man, Makoto went ahead and dragged the bodies of the manager and other employees out from behind the counter.

Shusaku started working on the computer, following the instructions in the manual.

While he was doing that, Makoto went back out onto the floor and checked the location of the cameras. He also checked to see whether the water was still running, then grabbed two microwavable bento lunches and popped them into the microwave. Unwrapping a rice ball, he began to nibble at it while he rifled through the beverages. He selected two colas and two oolong teas and carried them back to the staff room.

"Which do you want, cola or tea?"

"Sprite," said Shusaku, still tapping away at the keyboard.

"That wasn't one of the options," retorted Makoto, finally smiling for the first time. He went back to the fridge and brought Shusaku a sprite. "Here."

"Thanks."

"You find the footage?"

"It's coming up now."

Ding, chimed the microwave.

"You want a bento?"

"Yeah. One with a croquette in it, preferably."

"You can have the nori bento, then. I'll have the salmon," said Makoto. He opened the microwave and took out the two bentos, then glanced around. "If I were chopsticks, where would I be...?"

He finally found them and grabbed two pairs. By the time he returned to the staff room, Shusaku was getting ready to input the time for the surveillance footage.

"When should we start?" he asked.

"It was probably around 8:30 when the planes crashed," Makoto replied.

"Sounds right."

"So let's start five minutes before that. We need to get a clear picture of what happened."

"Got it."

Shusaku entered 12/25, 8:25 PM. The footage began to play.

The two employees were chit-chatting with each other. Apparently the cameras had microphones as well.

The store manager, meanwhile, was on the phone. They could hear him saying, "Go to sleep, little baby, daddy loves you too." Looked like the manager had a kid.

On one of the other cameras they could see a man who looked to be in his thirties, leering at the adult section of the magazine rack while he waited for the bathroom. They hadn't checked the bathroom, but that meant there was probably another body inside.

Makoto unwrapped his bento and removed the lid. Shusaku did the same, and the two began to poke at their microwaved meals while the footage continued to play.

"How is it?" asked Makoto.

"I'd rather be eating my mother's croquettes."

"Your mom's croquettes are gross."

"Maybe you'd rather eat my fist."

"To be honest, I'd rather be eating your mom's croquettes right now, too."

"Yeah… Yeah."

The same forlorn feeling gripped both boys.

They continued watching the tape as they ate.

Finally the timestamp reached 8:30 p.m.

But nothing happened.

8:35.

Still nothing.

8:39.

Movement.

The bathroom door opened and a little girl of seven or eight emerged.

"Took you long enough," said the man who had been ogling the adult magazines.

"Dad!"

"Did you wash your hands?"

"Of course I did, dummy!"

"Language! What would your mother say if she heard you talking like that?"

"It's your fault for being a dummy! Everybody could hear you!"

She had a point, everybody *could* hear him.

And then the timestamp reached 8:40.

Suddenly, the father's body began to twitch. On the other cameras, the manager, employees, and other customers likewise began to convulse with pain, blood spilling from their mouths and noses.

"D… Daddy?!" the little girl shouted, "Daddy, stop it! That's not funny!"

The girl's father realized something was wrong. Behind him, another man coughed up a spray of blood and keeled over. The father spun around and stared at him, clutching at his own chest.

"I-It hurts... M-Misa...!" he cried, whirling back to face his daughter. She seemed to be unaffected, however, and they could see the obvious relief written on the man's face in that moment, even as he vomited blood. "Misa, get away from me!" he shouted. "You'll be infected!"

"Daddy!"

"The bathroom! Go hide in the bathroom! Wait for..." A huge gush of blood erupted from his mouth.

"Daddyyyyyy!" the girl screamed.

Before she could get any closer, however, the man grabbed a handful of adult magazines from the nearby rack and hurled them at the girl.

She trembled, froze, then began to wail. "Wah...waahhhhh...!" She did as she was told, however, running back to the bathroom instead of towards her father. The door shut behind her, and the lock clicked.

Makoto and Shusaku exchanged glances.

"It doesn't affect kids!" Shusaku exclaimed.

"Stop the video!" cried Makoto. "There's a survivor!"

Makoto left the staff room, leapt over the counter, and headed towards the bathroom. The father lay dead beside the adult magazines. He had died protecting his daughter. By throwing porno mags at her head.

The magazines still lay on the floor in front of the fridge.

Makoto approached the bathroom, and opened the door.

"..."

But there was no one inside.

The little girl was gone.

"Tsk. She must have left." He should have expected that. It had been over an hour since she first locked herself in there.

He went back to the staff room.

"The girl?" asked Shusaku.

"Gone."

"Must've left."

"Start the tape again. Shusaku."

"Yeah?"

"It may not affect kids, but did you see any kids on our way here?"

"Nope. No kids, alive or dead."

"So where did they all go?"

"…For now, let's just watch the tape," suggested Shusaku, pressing PLAY again.

But nothing else happened.

Ten minutes passed, and still nothing. They could hear the girl sobbing in the bathroom, but that was it.

Twenty minutes, and still nothing. Just the girl's voice, calling for her mommy and daddy.

Forty minutes. Still nothing. They could hear the girl calling for help, but nothing more.

Finally, forty-three minutes later, the cameras picked up a sound coming from outside the store.

Hweeeeek! A strange, high-pitched howl.

"Who's there?" the girl asked. "Is someone out there? Can you help me?"

The door to the bathroom opened, and the girl came out into the store. When she spotted her father's body, her face crumpled again and tears spilled down her cheeks.

"Daddy…" she whimpered, but she abided by her father's command and didn't approach his body. Instead she made a detour, exiting the store by way of an aisle with no bodies in it. Smart girl.

Hweeeeek! Outside, the sound continued.

Hweeweek!

Hweeeeek!

It almost sounded like the cry of an animal.

And then—"Aieeeeee!" the girl screamed in terror. "Nooo! Noooooo!!"

She bolted back into the store. A few seconds later, a bizarre creature followed her in. The thing's monstrous body was white, with spindly insectoid legs, and arms that ended in wicked sickles like those of a praying mantis. It was three times the size of a human being, and it was hard on the girl's heels, pursuing her with murderous intent.

The girl tripped over one of the corpses and fell with a scream.

Hweeeeek! The creature let loose a tremendous roar, raising its right appendage in the air. The sickle began to descend upon the girl.

And then, suddenly, the creature had no head.

A man appeared out of nowhere, and lopped off the creature's head with a single stroke of his sword. He was beautiful, tall, with brown hair. Probably not Japanese.

The monster was dead. They had no idea what the strange white creature was, but more importantly...

"An adult. He's an adult," Shusaku observed. "Does that mean not everyone was infected?"

The man in the video spoke. "Pest," he muttered, "you're in the way," and grabbed the monster's carcass, flinging it out the door as if it weighed nothing.

The little girl stared at him as if he were the messiah, and stammered, "A-Are you here to save me?"

The man looked down at her. His eyes were red. Pure red. Not bloodshot, but a beautiful crimson. "Eh? Why would I save cattle?" he asked, staring down at her with those beautiful red eyes.

"Huh?"

Just then, the cameras picked up another voice, coming from behind the man. It sounded like it was coming through some sort of loudspeaker.

"Attention! The foolish humans have released a deadly virus! Regrettably, the human race has fallen! However, it appears as if children under the age of thirteen have not been affected. By the authority of Lucal Wesker, Progenitor of the Fifteenth Rank, we hereby place the children of this area under our care and supervision."

"Fallen...?" The little girl's voice shook, her face contorted with fear. She glanced up at the man in desperation. "But you'll protect me?"

"We've got to conserve our food supply," the man replied. "Thanks to the stupidity of the humans, there won't be much blood to go around anymore. I guess I'd better drink up now, while I have the chance."

He grabbed the girl.

"B...B...But..."

As she stammered her confusion, the man opened his mouth wide, revealing a pair of fangs. He clamped his mouth onto the girl's neck and began sucking out her blood. Makoto and Shusaku watched as the girl's life force faded away before their eyes.

"Phew!" The man opened his mouth, releasing her neck with a satisfied smack.

He was a vampire.

A real vampire.

Makoto's magic instructor had told him that vampires existed, and that they were unnaturally strong. "If you ever encounter one, keep your distance," he had said. "Never approach a vampire, under any circumstances." But Makoto had assumed the whole thing was just an old wives' tale.

Now, however, he was watching a real live vampire attack that girl on the screen.

It looked as though she was still alive, but she wasn't moving.

"Are you dead?" the man asked.

" . . . "

"Oh well, not that it matters. Oi, you there," called the man, speaking to someone behind him.

"Yes, sir?" Another man entered the store, attired similarly to the first. He was wearing a white uniform. A vampire's uniform.

"I think this one's still alive. Put her in the pen with the other cattle."

"Did you drink her blood?"

"You should have some too. It'll be our little secret from Lord Lucal."

"If we take any more from this one she'll die. I'm fine, I already drank from several of the children on the truck."

"If we don't bring in enough children, Lord Lucal will be angry."

"None of my unit killed any of them, so we've already reached our quota. Let's take this one in alive as well."

The two vampires scooped up the little girl and left the store.

And that was that.

Makoto and Shusaku fast-forwarded through the rest of the footage, but nothing else happened until they saw themselves entering the convenience store.

They stopped the video.

" . . . "

" … "

The two sat in silence for a while.

Now they knew why they hadn't seen any children.

The vampires were rounding them up like livestock. Because so much of the human race was dead. Everyone over the age of thirteen was gone.

The only reason Makoto and Shusaku were still alive was that they were still eleven years old.

The adults were all dead.

And vampires were rounding up the children.

There was also the question of the strange, white insectoid monsters that were attacking the surviving children. What were those things?

Though that paled in comparison to the question of why all of this was happening in the first place.

"He said the human race had fallen," breathed Makoto.

Shusaku nodded. "Yes, he did."

"Do you think it's true?"

"I don't know, but things look really bad."

"Do you think all the adults at home are dead, too?"

" … "

Shusaku looked over at Makoto. He still looked hopeful.

Makoto hadn't given up yet, either. The sorcerers of the Imperial Moon were smart. They lived by a spartan code, unflaggingly strong and committed to their training. Perhaps they had even foreseen what was coming.

Then again…

" … "

Makoto folded his arms in thought. He stared at the image frozen on the screen, of himself and Shusaku as they entered the convenience store.

He could see the fear in his own face.

The boy on the screen certainly didn't look like he was keeping his cool. Makoto needed to be stronger than that. He was a member of the Order of the Imperial Moon, a sorcerer in the service of Lord Guren himself. He had to be strong.

"..."

He remembered the conversation he'd had with his father before heading into the mountains. He'd been pretty fired up at the time, hell-bent on ramping up his training after his meeting with Lord Guren.

His father had seemed pleased at the time. Or thoughtful, perhaps.

Why don't you go up into the mountains for a little while, then? he had said. *If you really want to reach those heights, you need to spend some time coming face to face with yourself. And while you're doing that, I'll have your instructors update your training regimen. You can take Shusaku with you. How does that sound?*

It had seemed like a good idea, so that was exactly what Makoto had done.

That was five days ago.

Maybe his father had known all along what was going to happen. Maybe not. Makoto had no way of being sure. But if his father *had* known, and he had sent Makoto into the mountains to escape—

Shusaku interrupted his thoughts. "My mother made me croquettes when she came home. She even asked me how I liked them. She hardly ever cooks for me even when she comes home from a trip. She always says she's no good at it. And it was so sudden, too. She wasn't supposed to be back for a while."

The way Shusaku described it, it almost sounded like she had made him croquettes because she knew it was the last time they would see each other.

Had Shien and Makoto's father both known what was going to happen?

Maybe they had been making plans all along for what was coming, and sending their kids away was part of that.

If they had known it was coming, that is.

"We'll know more about what's going on once we get home," said Makoto.

"Right, let's go."

"We can't go straight there, though."

"'Course not."

After all, the streets were full of vampires.

And those mysterious monsters. Those creatures were fast, one glimpse was enough to see that. If they encountered one they would have no way of fighting it. Let alone a vampire, who could dispatch one of the monsters in the blink of an eye.

Their only chance was to stick to cover and avoid detection. To tread ever so cautiously, with bated breath—hiding in the shadows the whole way home.

"It'll probably take a few days," said Makoto.

Shusaku reached into his knapsack and took out his spare clothes. "We should fill our packs with food. We can get new clothes once we make it home."

"Right."

"If all the adults are dead but some of the children are still alive and in hiding, there'll be competition for supplies at the convenience stores and supermarkets. We should take everything we need now."

Makoto started dumping his own clothes from his knapsack. "I think it'll probably take us about six days to get home," he said.

They could be there in half a day at a steady run, but it would take much longer traveling cautiously.

Shusaku nodded. He grabbed a pen and began jotting down notes in a notebook that was sitting nearby. "We should prepare supplies for eight days. We'll need food, batteries, water—"

"You make the list," interjected Makoto, and left the staff room, circling around to the other side of the counter. He scanned the area intently, searching for any sign of enemies. He wasn't sure there was much point to it, though. Any enemy they did encounter would be stronger than them. The moment Makoto and Shusaku were detected, it would be lights out.

Which was exactly why they had to tread cautiously.

Makoto exited the convenience store. Off to the side, a little way away from the entrance, lay the body of the monster from the video.

"Holy shit," he breathed, staring down at it.

Makoto wasn't sure whether or not it was safe to approach the thing. For all he knew, it could be the source of the virus.

He took a few steps closer anyway.

"Holy shit," he said again.

"Makoto," came a voice from behind him. Shusaku had come outside as well. He grabbed Makoto by the arm, pulling him back before he could get any closer to the creature. "Let's go home, Makoto. Everyone's probably waiting for us."

Makoto wasn't so sure.

But he prayed they were.

He crossed his fingers, and went back to gathering supplies.

Guren Ichinose: Resurrection at Nineteen

◆

In the end, it only took them four days to reach home.

At first the boys moved cautiously and their progress was slow, but they soon grew accustomed to this new world.

Running away from the vampires was easy.

They were blasting out those announcements via loudspeakers, calling the children to come to them for their own protection. Any time Makoto and Shusaku heard them in the distance, they just moved in the other direction. Or headed to the upper floors of a nearby building.

The vampires didn't even seem to be trying that hard. They were just grabbing what children they could and loading them onto trucks like cattle.

In truth, the kids who didn't get captured were the ones getting the short end of the stick. The vampires may not have been trying hard, but the roving monsters were relentless. They pursued and slaughtered any human children they found.

The children tried to run, screaming and sobbing, but the monsters always caught them in the end. The smarter children hid; they knew if they got too close to the monsters they'd be killed. Eventually, though, they would need food and water. With the monsters about, how were they supposed to replenish their supplies?

The children Makoto and Shusaku did encounter seemed almost as scared of them as of the monsters. The youngest ones were already growing weak. Makoto and Shusaku shared food and water with them, but in the end they had to leave them behind and continue on their way.

It was hard to abandon them like that. They knew the children wouldn't survive long if left to fend for themselves. They were just normal kids. They hadn't spent their lives training, like Makoto and Shusaku had.

They found one little girl, six years old, sitting next to the body of her mother. She was weeping, and cradling a baby in her arms. The girl begged them to help her, but there was nothing Makoto and Shusaku could do. If they brought a screaming baby along with them, the monsters were sure to find them in no time. And then they would all be killed.

In the end, the only thing they could do was advise the girl to let the vampires take her. Who knew what awaited the children who were captured—life as a head of human cattle was probably unimaginably bleak—but at least it was better than certain death.

Because once you were dead, that was it.

All three of them were still just children. If they could just make it through this, they had their whole futures to look forward to.

" ... "

Makoto and Shusaku watched as the baby and little girl were taken away by the vampires.

On the move again—Makoto and Shusaku encountered three kids around their own age who were protecting a group of younger children.

Their names were Taro Kagiyama, Rika Inoue, and Yayoi Endo.

The three were gathering together surviving children, feeding them and keeping them hidden.

If only Makoto and Shusaku had met the three kids earlier, they might not have had to send that little girl and baby into the arms of the vampires. Unless, of course, without help these three were destined to die as well. If so, the girl and baby would have died with them. In which case they were better off with the vampires after all.

Makoto and Shusaku traveled with them for a short while, before finally going their separate ways. "We're going to a place where there might still be grown-ups. If there are, we'll come back for you," Makoto promised.

"You better! You promised!" insisted Rika. She almost sounded angry.

The kids all looked ready to cry.

Makoto couldn't blame them. Even with all his training, Makoto wanted to cry too. He reaffirmed the promise once more before departing.

But he had no way of knowing whether it was a promise he'd be able to keep.

They were moving at a much faster pace now, having figured out by this point how to avoid the vampires and insect monsters.

Four days later, they finally reached home.

"..."

The house was in total disarray.

The adults were all dead—but it didn't look as if they had died from the virus.

They had clearly died in battle.

Many of the bodies weren't wearing Imperial Moon regimentals; they were dressed in a different combat uniform. There had been casualties on both sides, slain by sword wounds to their chests and necks.

"These uniforms belong to the Order of the Imperial Demons," Shusaku observed.

The Imperial Demons, led by the Hiragi Clan. The house had been attacked by Imperial Demon troops.

So war had broken out after all.

"Does that mean someone released a biological weapon as part of the war?" Makoto asked. "And did my father and Shien know this war was coming?"

But Shusaku didn't know any more than he did.

Their only choice was to proceed deeper into the house.

This was Shusaku's home. Built in the Japanese style, it was large enough to be considered a manor by most people's standards.

The two continued onward.

There was no trace of Shien, however. While the fighting seemed to have reached every corner of the house, Shusaku's mother was nowhere to be found—living or dead. Of course, it was possible that her body was buried under the countless other corpses heaped throughout the house.

"Mother," breathed Shusaku, in a voice so quiet Makoto could barely hear it.

But such stealth was necessary. If there were still enemies nearby, any sound could give away the boys' location.

Makoto put his hand gently on Shusaku's back.

Shusaku turned to look at him. "Sorry, I'm alright," he said.

Makoto smiled weakly. "That makes one of us."

"You...want me to pat you on the back too...?"

"Uh huh."

Shusaku patted him on the back. Amid the overwhelming carnage, that moment of contact was the only thing that helped remind them they were still alive.

"Shien isn't here," said Makoto.

"With this many bodies, it's impossible to tell."

Makoto glanced toward the blood-splattered living room. He and Shusaku had played together in that room countless times. The nanny who took care of them had always been kind and gentle, and had never scolded them no matter what they got up to. Now she was lying there dead on the floor.

"…"

Makoto stared at her body.

And there, next to her on the tatami mat, he caught sight of a footprint in the dried blood.

Was it made after the virus spread? Or after the battle, but before the doom the virus had wrought?

Makoto grabbed Shusaku's arm and pointed at the print.

Shusaku gasped and moved closer, crouching down beside it. "It's big. Definitely belongs to an adult."

"Could it have been a vampire?" Makoto wondered aloud.

Shusaku glanced up at him. "There were no children here. Judging from what we've seen, I don't think the vampires would have bothered coming all this way."

Makoto agreed. The vampires didn't seem particularly motivated. They could barely be bothered, even when there were children to be "protected" right in front of them.

Then…

"Who made this footprint?" asked Makoto.

"It could've been made during the battle," replied Shusaku, but they both knew they were hoping for something else.

"But if it wasn't…" began Makoto.

"…"

"If it was made after the virus spread, then at least one adult survived."

The two boys followed the footprints. They trailed off as the bloodstains came to an end, but it was clear where they were headed.

Toward Makoto's house.

Makoto's house was in the same state as Shusaku's.

It had been laid waste by a fierce battle, half the roof caved in almost as if it had been hit by a missile.

And the interior was again littered with corpses.

Corpses in Imperial Moon uniforms.

And corpses in Imperial Demons uniforms.

"Shusaku, do you see what I see?" asked Makoto.

"Yeah, I see it," nodded Shusaku.

"Tell me what you see."

"You say it first."

"No, you say it first. I don't want to say it if it's not the same thing."

"All of the bodies have external wounds," offered Shusaku. "It doesn't look like anybody here died from the virus."

Which meant that they had all died during the fight. And if that was true...

"...my father and Shien might still be alive."

Shusaku inhaled quietly. There was hope. There was still hope.

Makoto headed toward his father's study. The room held a desk, and a bookshelf filled with difficult magical formulae and important tomes on leadership.

Among them was one of his father's favorite books, which he had reread numerous times. Makoto took it down from the shelf, and flipped through the pages before tossing it onto the floor.

Next he grabbed a book that his father had once recommended Makoto read. He flipped through the pages, then tossed it to the floor beside the first one.

Then he forced open the locked drawer in his father's desk. There were several papers inside, as well as a photograph of Makoto's mother, who had died when he was three.

Makoto didn't actually remember much about his mother, but his father had told him several times that she had been a powerful sorceress. Strong enough to go toe-to-toe with Shien, even, which is where his father said Makoto got his talent for magic.

From what he had heard, his mother died in the line of duty.

"What are you looking for, Makoto?" asked Shusaku from behind.

"I don't know…"

"You think there'll be some clue about what happened?"

"Maybe. I'm not sure, but…"

"But what?"

"My dad said that if anything ever happened, he'd leave a note for me in his favorite book."

Shusaku glanced down at the books on the floor. "But you didn't find anything?"

"Nothing."

"Let's check the other books, then." Shusaku began rummaging through the bookshelf.

After checking the desk thoroughly, Makoto sat down in his father's chair. It was still too large for his eleven-year-old body.

Makoto had always wanted to grow up to be like his father someday. His father knew everything. He was strong and firm, but also kind.

Or at least, that was how he had seemed to the young Makoto.

Still sitting in his father's chair, Makoto scanned the room.

There was a picture hanging on the wall.

Makoto had drawn it when he was two, back when his mother

was still alive. The drawing was terrible, and even he couldn't make out what it was meant to be—but according to his father, he had said it was a rocket when he drew it.

Makoto stood up, and took the picture off the wall.

Shusaku glanced his way, but continued flipping through books and tossing them on the floor.

Makoto turned the picture over. He removed the backing board and pulled the picture out of the frame. Staring at it now, he still couldn't see the rocket. He might've said that was what it was, but he had clearly been trying to draw a frog. Look, there was a green body, and those were four legs coming off of it.

"..."

It didn't matter either way. Makoto didn't care about the picture. It might've meant something to his father, but it didn't mean anything to him.

Makoto turned the picture over.

There was a drawing on the back as well. This one was easier to identify—it was of his mother.

Makoto remembered drawing this one. Specifically, he remembered how happy his mother had been when he showed it to her. Makoto had barely any memories of his mother, but the joyful hug she gave him when he drew this picture was one thing he did remember.

His father had seemed happy, too.

And there, in one corner of the paper.

"..."

Next to that terrible drawing of his mother.

"Shusaku... I found something."

"What?!"

"A secret message."

"You're kidding!"

Shusaku rushed over in excitement and stood next to Makoto.

They stared together at the drawing of Makoto's dead mother. Something had been scrawled beside the picture in Makoto's father's hand.

I have my task. What's yours?

Makoto and Shusaku exchanged another glance.

"I wonder when he wrote it," said Shusaku.

"The meaning seems intentionally unclear, and it doesn't say who it's for. He must have suspected it might fall into the wrong hands."

"So it really is a secret message."

"I think so."

"What do you think your father's 'task' is?"

"I don't know. But apparently mine's different. My father's got his task, and I've got my own."

His father had been sure that this message would be enough.

Enough for Makoto to understand what he wanted to get across.

And it was. He knew now what his task was to be.

There was one thing Makoto should be focusing on above all else. Why hadn't he thought of it sooner?

"Shusaku."

"Yeah?"

"Lord Guren is still alive. We're going to Tokyo."

Voices.

Both male and female.

"Wakey-wakey, Guren. Come on, sleepyhead."

"..."

"Guren, quit fooling around! Seriously, wake up already!"

"..."

"Hey, Guren! Wake up, man! Shit is crazy out there. I mean real crazy."

"..."

"Everyone, please, stop trying to wake Master Guren. I'm sure he's exhausted."

"..."

"Are you sure Master Guren isn't just trapped underneath your boobs, Sayuri? With his head in your lap like that, they're right on his face."

"No way. Is that true, Master Guren?"

Despite this raucous chorus, Guren wasn't coming to.

He didn't want to wake up.

He just wanted to sleep forever.

His mind felt foggy. But they just kept right on talking.

"Dude, seriously. I'm telling you, it's crazy! I mean, yeah, it's like a zombie movie outside, but I'm talking about Sayuri's boobs. They're massive!"

"Norito! This is no time for your pervy jokes!"

"But look at them, Mito. Have you ever seen anything like it?"

"I mean, th-they're not that... That is, mine aren't exactly small, either..."

"Wanna show me?"

"Of course I'm not going to show you! Besides, this is NO! TIME! FOR! YOUR! PERVY! JOKES!"

How could anyone be so loud? It felt like they were shouting right into his ear.

"Geez, would you guys shut up..."

Guren was finally coming around.

His eyes opened a crack.

At first the world was blindingly bright, and he couldn't see a thing. He clenched his eyes shut for a moment, then opened them again.

That did the trick.

When Guren opened his eyes, he discovered a world full of light and joy.

A world where his friends—his family—were alive.

Shinya, Norito, Mito, Shigure, and Sayuri were peering down at him with worried expressions.

They were alive. All five of them were alive.

Unless he was dreaming, they were healthy and whole and staring at him expectantly. It was the most reassuring sight Guren could have imagined.

"Good morning, Sleeping Beauty," said Shinya, grinning down

at him.

Beside him, Mito furrowed her brow. "There's nothing good about it, Lord Shinya. Guren, you've been asleep for way too long. The situation is serious!"

Norito nodded. "She's right, Guren. Sayuri's ginormous boobs have been sitting on top of your head this entire time!"

"They still are," put in Sayuri with a grin.

"If they're too heavy, just let me know and I'll adjust them," said Shigure, reaching for Sayuri's breasts with both hands, a serious expression on her face. "Unless they feel good. If they feel good, I suppose I'll have to leave them there."

"They are a little heavy," replied Guren.

"Preparing to lift boobs," said Shigure, hoisting up Sayuri's breasts with a grunt.

"Yuki!" Sayuri exclaimed.

"This is no time for goofing around!" interrupted Mito angrily. She grabbed Guren by the arm and dragged him forcefully to his feet.

His body felt so heavy. Why? Slowly, it all came back to him.

The anesthetic.

After hiding his friends on the top floor of a building, he had injected himself in the neck with it.

An extra-large dose.

It had been enough to kill several dozen ordinary humans. Hell, it probably would've been enough to kill an elephant. In other words, enough to still take effect despite the demonic strength coursing through Guren's body. That was why he was having such a hard time clearing his head.

He managed to stand up with Mito's help, but his legs wobbled beneath him.

"Master Guren!"

"Master Guren!"

His two retainers cried out in concern, but he managed to stay erect with Mito's help. "Geez, Guren, are you sure you're alright?" she asked, her face also clouding with worry.

"I feel a little dizzy," he said, putting a hand to his head. "What happened?"

When he was able to look up again, Shinya and Norito were standing before him. "We don't know yet," Shinya replied. "When we woke up, we were here."

Namely, on the 22nd floor of a high-rise in Shinjuku, in an office belonging to a company called Sential. The workers had all left for the day before anything happened, and the office was empty.

Guren had dragged Shinya and the others there before administering his own dose of anesthetic. He couldn't leave them outside—there were strange white monsters roaming the streets, hunting humans.

Guren felt it instinctively the moment he saw the creatures: they were another form of divine punishment meted out to the sinful human race. They looked like bizarre insects, yet there was something almost noble about them.

Guren had witnessed several demon-possessed survivors from the ranks of the Order of the Imperial Demons fighting one of them at the main intersection in Shinjuku. The battle had been fierce, and many of the soldiers had died.

Apparently the monsters were stronger than the power of the demonic curse, so leaving his friends outside when he injected himself with the anesthetic was not an option. Instead he had labored to hide everyone inside this building.

"Where are we?" Guren asked, looking around the room,

though he knew the answer perfectly well.

"Some office building," answered Norito. "The real problem is what's going on outside."

"What do you mean?" Guren turned toward the window.

It was the middle of the day.

The sky was blue.

The sun shone down hot and bright, reflecting off the windows of the building across the street, from which protruded the wreck of a passenger plane.

But Guren had already seen all this. He had watched as plane after plane plummeted from the sky, bundles of steel stuffed full of corpses that fell like shooting stars, devastating the city below.

But...

"...What the hell happened?" he asked.

It was Shinya who answered. "Looks like the world ended while we were asleep."

Guren looked at him. "Wait, why was I asleep?"

"Who knows? I was out, too."

"You were?"

"Yes. And so was everyone else. When we woke up, it was the middle of the day."

"But when did we go to sleep?"

"Don't *you* remember?"

Guren pretended to consider this question.

Shinya was smart. Too smart. What if he saw through Guren's ruse? If he realized Guren was faking, it was all over. Shinya would be annihilated. So Guren tried to look as convincing as possible. "Uh-uh. My memory's got holes in it. This is weird. What's going on?"

"What's the last thing you remember?"

Again, Guren tried to look like he was thinking about it.

How much would Shinya and the others remember? They had all died at the same time, so their memories should all end at the same point. It would be suspicious if Guren was the only one whose memory didn't match up.

"Shit, why does my head hurt so bad?" Guren crouched down, clutching his head.

"Are you sure you're alright?" asked Mito worriedly.

"What the hell happened to us? Norito…"

"Yeah?"

"Do you remember anything?"

"Nope… That is, all our memories are gone," Norito said. "The last thing any of us remember is riding down in that elevator."

Which elevator was he referring to? The one leading to the laboratory where the resurrection experiments were being carried out? That would mean their last memories were from just before they were killed.

Guren contorted his face as if in pain, and asked, "What about you, Shinya?"

Shinya nodded. "Same. Do you remember anything else?"

"I…" Guren clutched his head again, grimacing so that his friends couldn't read his expression. That was what he most feared, but he couldn't let them figure that out. Luckily for Guren, his behavior made his friends worry about him for completely different reasons.

"I knew it, they must have done something special to Guren," said Mito. "That's why he woke up later than the rest of us."

"Lady Mahiru was there, too," added Norito. "What if she had something special up her sleeve for Guren?"

Shinya took a step closer. He peered worriedly into Guren's

face. "Did Mahiru do something to you?"

But Mahiru was dead.

Shinya and the others were the ones who'd had something done to them. Guren had violated the taboo and dragged them back from beyond the brink of death.

But he couldn't tell them that, so he just shook his head, and said, "I don't remember. I...don't even remember an elevator. The last thing I remember is fighting Kureto." He cradled his head in his hands once more.

"Something clearly happened to you," said Shinya. "Mahiru must have done it."

But it was Guren. Guren was the one who had done it.

"We should get you checked out. But there's something I need to tell you, Guren, and I want you to stay calm. Things are pretty bad outside, and there's no time to waste."

I already know what you're going to tell me, thought Guren. *I did that, too.*

But he just raised his eyes and looked blankly at Shinya.

Shinya, for his part, appeared tense. Guren could hardly blame him. How were you supposed to tell your friend about the end of the world?

Norito, Mito, Shigure, Sayuri—they all wore the same expression: they had to tell him something terrible, and they couldn't bear to do it.

But no matter how terrible things were outside, Guren knew none of it came close to how he felt on the inside. He had done the unspeakable, bringing his five friends back to life.

"What is it? What the hell happened?" he asked, still looking confused.

Shinya just stared at him.

Guren gauged Shinya's expression carefully, trying to decide how to react to what came next. Shinya was smart. If Guren laid it on too thick, it might make Shinya suspicious. And the sooner they all got on the same page, the less likely Shinya was to notice any discrepancies in their stories.

So Guren returned Shinya's gaze, weighing his options carefully. How should he play this?

He made his choice, and spoke before Shinya could say anything more.

"You can't mean…the world really ended?"

Mahiru had already told them that was what would happen. It's why they had been fighting so hard. They were trying to prevent the end of the world as they knew it.

Shinya said nothing. He just gestured toward the window with his eyes, as if to say *see for yourself.*

Guren stood up and walked toward the window.

He already knew what was waiting outside.

The world lay in ruin.

Everyone save for demons and children was now dead.

And it was Guren's fault.

All because he had resurrected the five people standing behind him right now.

"…"

One of the windows was covered in tinted film. Guren could see his own reflection in its glass.

The reflection of his face. A liar's face.

And behind him, he could see the reflections of his five friends.

Guren looked out.

It hadn't been a dream.

The world had ended.

Guren Ichinose: Resurrection at Nineteen

A great many buildings had collapsed and lay in ruins.

Whole neighborhoods were on fire.

The streets were piled with corpses.

And through it all, dressed in the uniform of the Imperial Demons, raced soldiers possessed by the cursed gear they wielded.

"The Imperial Demons survived?" Guren asked as he looked down at them.

"Looks like it," replied Shinya.

"So humankind fell, but the demons survived?"

"Well, that was what the Imperial Demons were trying to accomplish this whole time, after all."

"So this was all part of their plan?"

"Maybe. We haven't tried asking. Actually, we were waiting for you to wake up first, since we weren't sure if asking would get us killed." Shinya came and stood beside Guren. "Remember, we fled the Imperial Demons as traitors. So, what do you think? Now that the world has been destroyed, will they be willing to take us back into the fold, or will we always be traitors in their eyes?"

"How long ago did you guys wake up?" asked Guren, turning to look at his friends.

"About an hour ago," answered Mito. "Norito and Lord Shinya went outside to check things out, and when they came back—"

"I woke up?"

"It's super crazy out there," interrupted Norito, throwing up his hands. "Everyone's dead, even the hotties!"

Guren grimaced. "It doesn't sound too serious when you say it like that."

"Didn't you hear me, Guren, all the hotties are dead! Sayuri might be the only girl with double Ds left in the entire world. It's over! It's all over!"

"Well excuse me for not being a double D!" With that, Mito socked Norito.

Guren noticed that she didn't say anything about not being a hottie, though, so she must have considered herself one.

Shigure stared at them all skeptically.

"…"

Guren didn't know what was going on, but they were all acting like nothing had changed. Suddenly he found himself laughing.

"It's not funny," said Shinya, an exasperated expression on his face.

"I know… I know…"

"I guess there's nothing we can do about it now, though. The damage has been done."

"…"

"Damn, we came up short again. Didn't get to save the world."

"…"

Save the world? Guren was the one who had destroyed it.

"And on top of everything, there're those strange monsters rampaging through the streets. The Imperial Demons soldiers are desperately trying to deal with them, that's why they're all running around out there. Plus, the children survived, so there's them to worry about—"

"…"

"The vampires are trying to get ahold of the children, too, to ensure their food supply. We saw them slaughter a squad of Imperial Demons. It's nothing but bodies out there, as far as the eye can see."

"…So you were waiting for me to wake up?" asked Guren.

Shinya nodded. "We needed some time to get a handle on the situation anyway. So, what do we do? With the world the way it is, if we choose to run, we might be able to stay one step ahead of the

Imperial Demons. Most of their soldiers are dead, after all."

Guren nodded. "If we do run, we should head north."

Shibuya, to the south, was where the Imperial Demons had their headquarters. That was where they would start rebuilding. Assuming the vampires hadn't already destroyed them, of course.

"So you think we should run?" prompted Shinya.

Guren gave it some thought. The truth is, he had already run away. If he had really wanted to save the world, he should've let himself be killed back there in the laboratory.

He had nowhere left to run to.

"Even if we did run, then what?" said Guren. "The world has ended. Where could we possibly go?"

"So you think we should join up with the Imperial Demons and help rebuild? Well, that's what I expected you to say. At least—" Shinya looked out the window at the chaos below. "It looks like my dear brother Kureto could use our help."

Guren surveyed the scene through the window. "Remember, though, it's possible this was all part of the Imperial Demons' plan."

"True enough."

"But if so, to what end?"

"No idea."

"Do you think we'll find out if we join up with them in Shibuya?"

"Maybe. If it was my father who was behind it."

Tenri Hiragi, the patriarch of the Hiragi Clan.

The same man who had killed Guren's father.

"Of course, I'm just a foster child," added Shinya with a self-deprecating smile. "I've barely ever even seen dear old dad's face."

What about Kureto, then? He had claimed he couldn't stop the impending catastrophe either. He hadn't possessed sufficient skill.

That's why he had entrusted the job to Guren's team.

They were supposed to save the world.

To stop Mahiru.

Yet even Mahiru had been a pawn in the Imperial Demons' plan. What if even the resurrection—

"..."

Guren gazed at his friends.

What if all of this was part of someone else's plan?

The destruction *and* the rebirth?

Mahiru died believing she was finally free of the Imperial Demons' control. Guren had chosen to bring back Shinya and the others. But if their actions had actually been part of someone else's plan...

"..."

...then whoever this mastermind was, he needed to be killed. He was an enemy of the human race. Not that there were many people left in the world who could be called human anymore.

Gods? Devils?

Guren stared out the window at the streets below.

Peering at him from the side, Shinya said, "Hey, Guren?"

"Yeah?"

"Has your memory returned at all? Or is the last thing you remember still the fight with Kureto?"

Why was Shinya still asking about his memory? Weren't they done talking about that? Shinya must have been on to him, must have felt suspicious about Guren's memories ending at a different point than everyone else's.

In fact, Shinya had been giving Guren funny looks ever since he had woken up. He must have realized right away that Guren was hiding something.

Guren Ichinose: Resurrection at Nineteen

Of course Shinya noticed.

Shinya always noticed.

He caught every detail, no matter how minute or banal or trifling. There was little chance Guren would be able to keep a secret this big from him for long.

"…"

Which was why Guren had made his lie so obvious. The idea that he couldn't remember anything after the fight with Kureto was preposterous.

Guren glanced at Shinya.

His friend was staring at him with a mixture of worry and suspicion. As their eyes met, Shinya asked lightly, "So there's something you want to keep secret from us?"

Guren responded in a low voice. He needed to steer Shinya in some other direction so he wouldn't pursue the matter and discover the truth of their resurrection.

By sharing a different secret with him, for instance.

By making Shinya think that the furtive expression in his eyes was masking some other secret.

"I didn't want to tell you," whispered Guren.

"But you're going to anyways, right?"

"…"

"It's a little late to be keeping secrets from each other, don't you think?"

"…"

"Would you rather I got to the bottom of this little puzzle on my own? I'm not sure what the point of that would be, but if that's what you want—"

Guren cut him off. "I…killed Mahiru."

Shinya fell silent, his eyes widening just a little.

Guren could feel the others fall silent as well, their full attention on what he would say next. "Mahiru was in the elevator," he continued, not turning around. "She's the one who drugged all of you."

"..."

"She said that if I didn't kill her, she was going to kill Norito and Mito, and Shigure and Sayuri...and you, Shinya."

"She...wanted you to kill her?"

"Uh huh."

"Why?"

"Dunno."

"And you just did it?"

Guren paused for a beat before answering. "She was going to kill you guys."

"So that's how it was, huh. She was about to kill us, and you killed her to prevent it."

"..."

"So it's our fault. We're the reason you had to kill Mahiru."

"..."

"What'd she say at the end?"

"..."

"I have the right to know what she said before she died, don't I? I was her fiancé, after all," insisted Shinya.

Guren recalled what Mahiru had said just before she disappeared. "She said...that her pathetically weak idiot of a prince had finally caught up to her...and kissed her tainted, filthy demon lips..."

"Hnh... So did you cry?"

"What do you need to know that for?"

"I don't... But did you?"

"..."

"Of course," said Shinya, then repeated, "Of course…" Hopefully he was satisfied now. "So, what happened to her?" he asked.

There was no need for further lies. Mahiru's arms were wide enough to harbor every remaining secret. Guren could stick to the truth for the remainder of his story and trust that the enigma that was Mahiru would soak up the rest. If he could just clear this hurdle, he was home free.

"She disappeared," he answered truthfully. "She was absorbed into my katana."

Shinya looked over at the sword Noya where it hung at Guren's waist. "Absorbed? How?"

"I don't know. Noya… That is, the demon of this sword, said that he was being absorbed by Mahiru."

"Wait, it was the demon that was absorbed? Does it still speak to you?"

"No. Not right now, at least."

"Is the demon gone?"

"The voice is gone. But the power is still there, same as ever."

If anything, it felt even more powerful than before.

Hrm. Shinya laid a contemplative finger across his mouth. Then: "What was Mahiru after?"

"…I don't know." Which was the truth. Even now, Guren had no idea what Mahiru had been trying to accomplish.

"Do you think she was trying to merge with you, somehow?" asked Shinya.

"Maybe, who knows."

"Does *she* speak to you?"

"The sword isn't speaking at all. Total radio silence. I can't hear the demon or Mahiru…"

Yes. Silence.

He hadn't heard a word from Noya or Mahiru since Mahiru's disappearance.

And yet the sword continued to supply him with power.

"Then this could still be part of Mahiru's plan," said Shinya.

"..."

"The world has been destroyed. But we survived. No, someone made us survive. Gave us anesthetic, even." Shinya put a hand to his neck. The mark where the syringe had punctured his skin was already gone, but Guren wouldn't be surprised if Shinya could still feel that something was off.

It was Guren, however, who had injected Shinya with the anesthetic.

He glanced at Shinya's neck, and Shinya looked at his in turn. Guren froze.

Had the wound on his own neck healed? Where Ferid had bitten him?

Norito suddenly piped up from behind them. "Hold on, if Lady Mahiru disappeared, then who drugged Guren?"

"That's right," chimed in Mito. "Guren, had you already seen that the world—"

"No," Guren shook his head.

But it was a lie.

He had seen it.

The world had ended, and it was his own fault.

"I suddenly lost consciousness a little while after Mahiru was absorbed by the sword," he lied, "and, when I woke up, I was here."

His friends all exchanged worried glances.

"Then it's possible…" began Norito, "that Lady Mahiru actually took over your body, and that's why your memory is gone, isn't it?"

"Wait! Wait! That doesn't sound good at all!" cried Mito in a panic.

Shigure and Sayuri stepped forward.

Shigure grabbed his right arm and Sayuri took his left.

"Master Guren!"

"Master Guren, are you alright?"

Shinya peered closely at him. "Mahiru?"

"I'm not Mahiru…" Guren said, returning his gaze.

"How can you be sure?"

"…"

He couldn't. Mahiru had entered him somehow. Something was different, he knew that much, at least. There was something inside him now, entwined with him, and that something wasn't Noya.

So maybe he wasn't the same Guren he had been before.

He looked long and hard at Shinya, and then around at his other friends. "You're right… I can't be sure. I think I'm still me, but…"

Shinya suddenly summoned his rifle—the demon known as Byakkomaru. It was tipped with a wicked bayonet. Guren didn't know what Shinya and Byakkomaru had been saying to one another, but now Byakkomaru was pointed at Guren's face—

"It's decided then. We have to return to the Imperial Demons. It's our only option. Mahiru might take control of Guren at any moment. We have to conduct the proper tests to make sure that doesn't happen."

As Shinya spoke, Shigure was already placing Guren's arms into restraints. "I'm sorry, Master Guren."

Guren shook his head. "No, you're doing the right thing. You have to keep me bound."

Norito, meanwhile, touched him lightly on the back.

"I'll cast an illusion. Until the tests are over, you just sleep a while longer."

"Thanks, Norito…"

Norito began to work his magic. Guren didn't resist, and the illusion quickly began to take hold. "Want me to make it a sexy one?" Norito asked.

Mito punched him in the shoulder. "No sexy illusions!"

"Ow!"

Mito stepped closer, bringing her face near to Guren's. His consciousness was already fading, his mind going blank. The magic was working.

"Don't worry," Mito said to him, "We're going to fix this, I promise."

"But how can we go back to the Imperial Demons?" Sayuri said to Shinya. "We're fugitives, remember?"

"First things first," he replied, "we head to Shibuya and scope it out. We do know one thing. My brother Kureto is on our side. At least, I think he is."

"Are you sure? Can we really afford to trust the Hiragis…?"

But Guren couldn't hear the rest of what she said. His consciousness was fading. He wasn't worried, though. He knew he could rely on his friends to figure something out.

Which is why, just before his consciousness faded away completely, he said, "Norito…"

"Yeah?"

"Make it a sexy one."

"You got it!"

"Guren!" cried Mito angrily.

But Guren just laughed, and then he was gone.

◆

Guren Ichinose: Resurrection at Nineteen

Guren dreamed.

It wasn't a sexy dream. It was a lovely, tranquil dream.

Guren was sitting by a river—he was pretty sure it was the one where he had first met Mahiru. It was in his hometown, in Aichi Prefecture. The same river where he had spent so much time training in his youth.

The sun was already dipping below the horizon, and the sky had turned a startling crimson.

Guren had spent another day training, swinging his wooden sword this way and that.

But he was no longer a boy. He was pretty sure he was sixteen.

Across the river on the opposite bank sat Mahiru.

She was dressed in her school sailor uniform, bare legs dangling from her skirt and kicking at the surface of the river, sending sprays of water into the air.

Guren looked around and saw that his friends were also there.

Norito was trying to start a fire. Now Guren remembered! They were having a cookout. They had all gone down to the river that day to make curry.

Mito, Sayuri, and Shigure were preparing the food.

A little further off, Shinya was trying to put up the tent.

Glancing towards him, Shinya said, "C'mon, Guren, help out."

"You hear that?" Guren shouted across the river to Mahiru. "You help out, too."

But Mahiru just smiled and said nothing.

"I said help out!"

She smiled at him.

"Mahiru!"

She just kept on smiling.

"Guren! Gurennn!" shouted Norito.

"Yeah?"

"I can't get the fire started. This charcoal's damp."

"Should I bring more from home?" It wasn't far.

"Yeah, would you?"

Guren set off walking toward his family's home.

That day had been so tranquil, the weather so gorgeous. A perfect day for camping and a cookout.

When Guren arrived home, Shigure and Sayuri's parents were both there. They told him how happy they were to see him again.

Guren had no idea what the fuss was about, so he just nodded and began looking around for more charcoal. He was pretty sure there was some out in the shed.

As he was making his way across the garden, he ran into his father.

His father beamed at him. "Did you make some friends in Tokyo?"

"I guess. I mean, I don't know if I'd call those guys my friends."

"But you invited them to come home with you, so you guys must be pretty close, right?"

"Yeah, I guess you could say that."

"This is the first time you've ever had friends over, after all."

"It is?"

"And you look happy."

"I do?"

"You do."

"Maybe I am, at that."

"Well, as long as you're happy, I'm happy."

"Quit it, it's embarrassing."

"Hahaha."

"By the way, dad."

"Yeah?"

"Do you know where the charcoal is?"

"Good question…" His father was still smiling. Guren loved it when his father smiled. His respect for the man ran deep. "I think there might be some in the shed."

Guren walked past his dad and opened the shed. It was practically overflowing with charcoal.

"I found it!" he called out, stuffing some into a bag and tossing it over his shoulder. He headed back to the river.

On his way back, he met several followers of the Order of the Imperial Moon. They all bowed their heads as they greeted him. *Lord Guren, you're finally home! Now that you've returned to us, you can finally take over the leadership of the Imperial Moon.*

Everyone seemed to be in good spirits, enjoying the pleasant evening. Guren passed a group of children, all shouting at each other to get home before it grew dark. The comforting smell of someone cooking dinner suddenly reached his nose.

Guren arrived back at the river.

"What took you so long!" chided Norito.

Guren apologized, and together they lit the fire.

Shinya had finished putting up the tent and walked over at that point, carrying colas for them.

"Out of the way!" cried the ladies, setting the pot atop the newly stoked fire.

Shinya, Norito, and Guren took a step back and began sipping their cola.

It was delicious. The most delicious thing Guren had ever tasted.

"Ahh," Guren sighed. "I wish today could last forever." He really did.

"Me too," said Shinya beside him.

"Me three," added Norito.

On the far side of the river, Mahiru continued to smile.

The sun began to set, but the glow of the coals illuminated the surroundings.

"I wanna roast some marshmallows!" said Shinya.

Guren smiled. "Me too."

The rest of their friends chimed in.

"Count me in."

"Yes, please."

"Me too."

"Me three!"

They took the pot off the fire and began roasting marshmallows, smooshing them between graham crackers before popping them into their mouths. The curry wasn't even done yet.

Mahiru, meanwhile, just continued smiling at them.

"Mahiru?" Guren called.

"…"

"Why don't you join us? Don't you want a marshmallow?"

Mahiru's smiling lips parted, as if she were about to speak.

And then, suddenly, it was over.

Guren's peaceful interlude had ended all too soon.

◆

He awoke abruptly.

"Ugh…"

Guren opened his eyes.

He was in a classroom. He recognized it: it was one of the classrooms at First Shibuya High School.

Guren was bound to a chair in the middle of the room.

There was a blackboard on the wall in front of him.

The clock read 10:20 p.m.

Bright shards of moonlight filtered in through the broken glass of the window, borne on a cold December wind.

Guren stared out the window from where he sat restrained. The world really had come to an end. The scene outside the broken window made that perfectly clear.

Several dead bodies had been piled up in one corner of the room.

"Dammit... I guess I was just dreaming," said Guren, staring at the corpses.

Unless it was the other way around, and this was the dream. How wonderful that would be.

But it's the nightmares we never wake up from.

Good dreams always end too soon.

Guren looked around at the classroom.

"What am I doing here?" he muttered.

Just then the door at the front of the classroom slid open with a bang and a young man stepped inside. He was in fighting trim, his back tall and straight. He wore a katana at his waist, and was dressed in the combat uniform of the Imperial Demons.

It was Kureto.

Kureto Hiragi.

"Did you say you were dreaming?" he asked, fixing Guren with a steely gaze.

"..."

"What kind of dream was it?"

"A dreamlike dream," replied Guren, looking up at him.

"Oh? And what's that supposed to mean?"

"A dream of what the world was like before it was destroyed."

"Ah." Kureto shrugged.

Closing the door behind him, he slapped a single *fuda*—a paper charm inscribed with a spell—onto the door.

It was a barrier *fuda*. And a powerful one at that.

By placing it there, Kureto had activated a series of connected *fuda* that would prevent any sound from escaping the room.

Kureto walked across the room and stood before the blackboard. It was covered in notes from a chemistry class. They must have been written before the world ended.

Kureto glanced at them coldly before addressing Guren. "I thought I told you to prevent the end of the world."

"I failed," Guren replied.

"Worthless."

"That's right, worthless."

Kureto glared at him. "Don't be so quick to acknowledge it," he said, walking towards the chair where Guren sat.

"Where are Shinya and the others?" Guren asked.

"I killed them."

"Bullshit."

"I'm afraid not. What did you expect? Death awaits all who betray the Hiragi Clan."

"Then why are you still alive? You're the one who fed me information, and asked me to prevent the end. Wasn't that a betrayal?"

Kureto came to stand directly in front of Guren and stared down at him.

Guren returned his gaze. Kureto was exhausted, he could see it in his face.

"You look tired," said Guren. "Is it that bad out there?"

"It's bad. But we've begun rebuilding."

"Of course you have, since this destruction was part of the Hiragis' plan all along. I bet you had the plans for rebuilding ready to go from the start, too, didn't you?"

Kureto shook his head. "Yes and no. There's been a hitch."

"A hitch? What do you mean?"

"Monsters. We weren't expecting that, and the fools in charge of planning the reconstruction were all wiped out. Not that I had anything to do with any of that."

"I bet."

"Plus, the vampires are trying to abduct all the surviving children, and they're too strong for us to do much of anything about it."

"So?"

"So, those of us who are left are working overtime to restore basic utilities and get the area back into some semblance of order."

"Amazing. And who's in charge of these efforts?"

"I am."

"Then I'm sure you're very busy. Do you really have time to waste on me?"

In response, Kureto withdrew a syringe from an inside pocket. "I don't," he said, "which is why I'm going to inject you with this truth serum. Then you'll tell me everything I want to know."

"Truth serum won't work on me," Guren informed him. "The demon makes my metabolism—"

"Yes, I know. You forget, we're on the cutting edge of research into the demon's curse here. That's why Shinya brought you to me. He was hoping we could save you."

That's right. Shinya had brought Guren in because he was worried that his friend had fused with Mahiru.

"Did you already run the tests?" Guren asked.

"We did."

"And?"

Kureto furrowed his brow slightly. "And I discovered that there's someone whose research is even further along than my own."

Did he mean Mahiru? Had Mahiru outstripped her brother?

"What exactly do you mean?"

"The demon inside you has advanced to a stage beyond our current technology. With your version of the curse, you can draw even greater power from your demon while still maintaining your sanity. But we've been analyzing it and we're already close to unlocking its—"

"I don't care about any of that. Just tell me if Mahiru is in there."

"She's not," Kureto replied. "The only thing inside you is a demon."

"And Mahiru?"

"She's not there."

"But she disappeared. And my demon was afraid, he said that Mahiru was absorbing him—"

Kureto cut him off again. "Listen to me carefully. We've figured out what's happening to you. You're hallucinating."

"I'm... What...?"

"Your demon is making you hallucinate. Giving you pleasant dreams, showing you what you want to see."

"What the hell are you talking about?"

"I'm fairly certain you tried to save the world, and crossed swords with Mahiru in the process."

"..."

"And you killed her, but your mind couldn't handle it. The demon used that to worm its way in, and you lost control. You've been hallucinating ever since..."

"You're wrong. That's impossible. I'm not out of control."

"I'm sorry, but according to our readings you clearly are, even as we speak. You seem to be rational and sane, but you're well on your way to transforming into a demon for good. We're formulating a sedative for you."

"No! You've got it all wrong! I…"

"You lost control in that underground lab and went on a rampage."

"No way. I… I…"

It couldn't be. Guren had been in control this whole time. If his demon *had* gone on a rampage, he would have been strong enough to destroy their enemies and prevent the apocalypse that had destroyed the world.

That was precisely the problem. Guren had been too weak.

He hadn't been able to do anything at all to stop the end.

"…"

Unless…it had been Guren all along.

Had Guren lost control?

Who had really killed Shinya and the others—

"You tell me, then," Kureto cut into his thoughts. "What happened down there?"

Guren stared up at him.

"…"

Obviously Guren couldn't answer. He had to keep the truth to himself. Otherwise, Shinya and the others might find out they had been brought back to life, and then they would disappear forever.

"Answer me. What happened? Or do I need to use the truth serum?"

"Go ahead… I can only tell you what I saw. I killed Mahiru. And then Mahiru disappeared into me. That's the last thing I remember."

Kureto stared intently at Guren. He was silent for a moment, then tossed the syringe onto the floor. "I believe you, for now. The serum wouldn't have worked on you anyway."

"But you gave me something else, didn't you? Something to put me off my guard. You're trying to scare me, to make me believe that my demon has taken over."

But Kureto shook his head. "It's true that we drugged you. But I wasn't lying about your condition. Your demon is out of control. Your levels are off the charts. And yet somehow you remain sane. This represents a new stage of control for the demon curse. Total fusion. But how? Did Mahiru do this to you?"

Of course Mahiru had done it. Mahiru was responsible for everything that had happened.

"Regardless," continued Kureto, "if this was Mahiru's doing, she's our savior. The power of the demon curse will grow exponentially thanks to this discovery. With this, we might even be able to take on the vampires."

"Take on the vampires?"

"We have no choice. They're abducting the children—the future of the human race. Besides, I doubt they'll willingly forgive the organization that was behind the resurrection experiments."

Apparently, Kureto already knew that the resurrection experiments violated the taboo. Fortunately, he didn't seem to know who had actually been resurrected.

Or did he?

What if there had been surveillance cameras inside the laboratory, and Kureto had watched the whole thing?

Mahiru's whole life had gone according to the Hiragis' scheme. Was it possible that this whole ordeal, including the resurrection of Shinya and the others, had been another of their machinations?

"So where are Shinya and the others?" Guren asked again.

"They're in Harajuku," Kureto replied.

"Harajuku? You're beginning the reconstruction in Harajuku? Not Shibuya?"

"Our base is still in Shibuya," Kureto informed him.

"Then why…"

"You could hardly expect me to bring your team back into the fold without having this little chat with you first."

"…"

"This whole cataclysm seems to have been orchestrated by the Hiragis. Even Mahiru was just our father's lab rat in the end. Is that assessment correct?"

It was. Mahiru had indeed been a lab rat, her fate decided from the moment she was born. But when Guren arrived, Mahiru had been waiting for him. She had destroyed the surveillance cameras, and killed all the technicians. And there at the bitter end, she told Guren she had escaped the fate that had been laid out for her.

The question now was whether Kureto had somehow seen all of it happen.

Had Mahiru broken free in the end? Or were they still dancing to someone else's tune?

"…"

Guren gave it some thought, but he didn't have enough information. He didn't know what it was safe to say, or how he might make the best of his current situation.

For that matter, now that the world had been destroyed, he wasn't even sure what he ought to be striving for.

All he knew was that he had to play his cards close to the vest to prevent Shinya and the others from disappearing forever—for the moment, that was all that mattered.

"Kureto," said Guren.

"Yeah?"

"Who do you consider your enemy?"

"My enemy?"

"Yeah."

"I don't have enemies."

"Then what do you live for?"

"…"

"In a world like this, what goals could a person possibly have?"

Kureto seemed to think for a moment, then looked back toward Guren and said, "You still haven't gotten a good look at the situation outside, have you? It's dire. If we don't make a stand now, the human race will be wiped out."

"…"

"For the weak and powerless, I *am* the goal. The Order of the Imperial Demons will lead the human race out of this—"

"Ha! The Imperial Demons are the ones who destroyed the world in the first place."

Kureto shrugged. "That wasn't my doing. But it's still my responsibility. Such is the duty that comes with power."

"So it's about duty now?"

"Duty. And doing the right thing."

Kureto drew his sword from his waist. The blade crackled faintly with electricity.

Raimeiki—that was the name of Kureto's sword.

It housed a demon capable of unleashing lightning.

Kureto flicked his sword, and Guren's restraints fell away.

He glanced down at his newly freed hands. "Why did you do that?"

"You have your own duty to carry out," replied Kureto.

"My own responsibility to take, you mean?"

"Yes."

"So I'm supposed to join you, and save the world?"

"That's exactly what you're supposed to do."

"But the Imperial Demons are the ones who destroyed the world in the first place. And we don't even know what for. What was the point of all this?"

" . . . "

"Do *you* know what they were trying to accomplish?"

" . . . "

Kureto was silent.

"You don't, do you?" said Guren, staring into Kureto's face. "You don't know, and you still talk about doing the right thing? What a crock of shit. And what power do you really have? How can a powerless shmuck like you hope to take responsibility for—"

Kureto had heard enough. He swung his fist, and connected solidly with Guren's face.

Guren could probably have dodged it if he had wanted.

Instead, he just took the punch. He wanted to get hit. He was the one who had pulled the trigger that destroyed the world. Even if the outcome had been a foregone conclusion, he had still played his part.

Guren tasted blood in the corner of his mouth, but the power of the demon within him healed the cut instantly. Even the tortures of hell wouldn't leave a scratch on him.

He was a monster now, in both body and soul.

Guren narrowed his eyes and glared at Kureto. "What was the point of that?"

Kureto stared down at Guren's blood congealing on his fist, and

125

replied, "Doesn't it make you feel like a character in a teen drama?"

Guren laughed. "Maybe it would've, before all of this. But look around, the world is lying in ruins—"

"We'll rebuild it."

"Hnh."

"The Imperial Demons' power has also waned thanks to this cataclysm. My father's influence isn't what it used to be. This school isn't even under surveillance at the moment. So if you join me—"

Guren cut him off. "If I join you, what? Don't tell me you're planning to stage a rebellion."

" … "

"Is that what your goals amount to in the end? If so, then you never really gave two shits about the rest of the world, did you," spat Guren.

"I always choose the best course of action, that's all," said Kureto, staring at him coldly. "And I will continue to do so, world be damned."

"Well excuse me, your majesty."

"Now you've got it. It's a shame I don't have a ring for you to kiss."

Guren ignored Kureto's foolish remark and glanced towards the window.

He had caught a glimpse of movement outside.

"Somebody's there…" he started to say, but Kureto was already moving. He charged suddenly towards the window, his sword raised above his head.

"Wh—?!" He heard a woman's voice, but her gasp was cut short.

Raimeiki had run her through, killing her. Kureto's momentum carried him through the window, but he twisted in mid-air, just barely catching onto the window ledge before he fell.

The woman's body, meanwhile, dropped several stories to the ground below.

Kureto clambered back through the window and looked at Guren.

"What was that you said about not being watched?" said Guren, returning his gaze.

"By one very weak woman. Can you imagine surveillance being that lax before the fall? My father would've brought this building crashing down around our ears the moment we even contemplated something like this."

"So it's a secret that you're meeting with me?"

"Meeting with traitors doesn't have such good optics."

"So why are you doing it? You don't really plan to stage a rebellion, do you?" Guren asked.

"I told you," replied Kureto. "I always choose the best course of action. Always. And right now, in order to do that, I need you."

"Hnh."

"Unless you join me, you won't be allowed back to Shibuya."

"But you want me back, don't you?" said Guren, staring with half-lidded eyes at Kureto where he stood by the window.

Kureto raised his sword in response, and murmured, "Raimeiki, roar."

For an instant lightning raced down the blade and across Kureto's body. With a single step he closed the distance between them, propelling himself across the room to stand mere inches from Guren's face.

Kureto's demon was a black demon, the most difficult type of cursed gear to wield safely. Those who did learn to do so, however, were bestowed power far surpassing that provided by ordinary demons.

Kureto's blade was coming straight for Guren, aimed most probably at his neck.

Unperturbed, Guren didn't react immediately. In a fight between two black demon wielders, such a delay could prove fatal. If Kureto was serious, he could easily cut off Guren's head.

However.

"…"

Guren finally reached for his own sword. Even he was surprised at how fast it flew from its scabbard; he blocked Kureto's blow before it could reach his neck.

The two swords clashed loudly, and with their blades still crossed, Guren pushed back.

Kureto was instantly overpowered, and Raimeiki flew from his hands.

It spun through the air, straight into the blackboard. The moment the blade made contact it released the lightning pent up within, blowing a gaping hole in the wall before clattering to the floor.

Guren looked at the wall out of the corner of his eye.

"Do you see now, Guren?" Kureto said, still standing before him. "You have a duty to carry out."

"…"

"With great power comes—"

Guren cut him off. "What the hell is going on inside my body?"

"I told you, your demon is out of control."

"Then why can't I hear its voice?"

"Because it's already too far gone. But we've finished our analyses and developed a drug to bring the demon back under control. Suppressing the demons after letting them rampage like this will allow us to extract even more power from them than ever before. Once my soldiers and I take the drug, we'll grow even stronger,"

Kureto explained.

So Kureto wanted to let the demons run wild then bring them back under control, making the wielders stronger by fusing them even more fully with their demons?

It was madness—they were toying once more with God's taboos.

"That sounds like dangerous research."

Kureto nodded readily. "It is. Which is why I was always so critical of Mahiru—there's nothing to gain by proceeding at the cost of one's own sanity. But things are different, now. The world just ended," he said, gesturing toward the window.

Guren's eyes followed his pointing finger.

"The world is growing more dangerous by the minute," Kureto continued. "This is no time for us to sit around and twiddle our thumbs."

That reminded Guren of something Mahiru had said.

According to her, she was the hare. In the fable, the slow and steady tortoise won the race when the speedy hare got cocky and decided to take a break. But this story was different.

In this story, the hare raced ahead desperately; its legs could be worn to stumps, its heart might explode in its chest, and still it ran heedlessly on and on and on. She ran faster and faster, until no one could even see her anymore—

Which meant that the tortoises could no longer be tortoises. They needed to run as fast as they could, even if it cost them their sanity.

"And the drug?" Guren asked.

"We start mass production tonight," answered Kureto. "This is the prototype." He removed an ampoule and syringe from an inside pocket.

"But you haven't tried it yourself yet. You'd rather experiment on your underlings first—"

"Seven people died to get us this far. They were all volunteers, all committed to doing their part to save what's left of the world."

"…"

"We have children to protect. A civilization to rebuild."

"…"

"But the experimental data are insufficient, safety is still not guaranteed. The risk is still too great for the leadership to use it. However," Kureto flipped the syringe around and jammed it into his own neck.

"Hey!" But Guren was too late. He watched as the red fluid drained out of the syringe and into Kureto's neck.

"Ngh." A look of pain swept across Kureto's face, as the dark magic of the curse swirled around his neck and then began spreading to the rest of his body.

"Kureto."

Kureto looked at him from behind a mask of pain. "If I lose control, cut off my head."

"Dammit, Kureto!"

"Urgh…" Kureto groaned in pain. Then, "Enough."

The curse stopped spreading, and shot smoothly back toward the spot on Kureto's neck where he had inserted the syringe.

Kureto grinned. "Success."

Guren rolled his eyes. "I'm starting to wonder if you're fit to lead."

"You're one to talk."

"…"

"Now listen, Guren, we don't have much time. Every moment we tarry, another child dies. It's up to us to stop it. Raimeiki, come."

Kureto summoned his demon quietly. The sword flew back to his hand, and he swung it at Guren again.

To the casual observer it might have looked like a relaxed swing, but Guren could see there was far more power behind it than Kureto had possessed before.

This time he reacted immediately. He could sense that if he didn't, he would be unable to fend off the blow in time.

"Noya," Guren called his own demon's name.

No response. The demon inside him didn't answer.

But it still supplied him with power.

The question was whether it would be enough to match Raimeiki.

Kureto's blade descended; Guren blocked it with his own.

The first time their blades met, Guren could feel how evenly matched they were.

When they met again, however, Guren noticed he had a slight edge over Kureto—but it was so slight that the outcome of their battle would come down to a combination of skill and luck. Or was it just that Guren's own demon was still rampaging out of control?

They crossed blades seven more times before Kureto finally took a step back.

"Such power," he said, gazing at the lightning that danced along Raimeiki's blade. "With this much power even the vampires won't be able to stand in our way."

It seemed to Guren that Kureto was overstating the case. At the very least, the difference in power hadn't done him any good against Ferid.

Then again, with a good battle formation, and the right strategy—

Guren returned his sword to its sheath. "—What about the nobles?" he asked.

Kureto looked at him. "There are different ranks even within the vampire nobility. Apparently their power increases drastically the higher they rise. Fortunately, the vampires' main headquarters is located to the west. There aren't many high-ranking nobles around Tokyo, so we should be able to retake the city."

It seemed Kureto had already begun gathering intel on the vampires. Though the Imperial Demons had probably been researching the vampires for some time, given that they'd had to keep their experiments into human resurrection—the Seraph of the End project—secret from the creatures.

Guren looked at Kureto. It seemed he really did intend to rebuild.

Even after everything that had happened, he hadn't given up. No complaints, no hesitation—just ready to rise to whatever challenge came next.

Guren took a breath. A deep one. Why was he here? After everything he had done, what was he to do with the rest of this life he had blundered into?

"..."

Kureto produced another syringe. "I want you to take the drug too. You'll be able to talk to your demon again once you do. The ability to talk to your demon is proof that you're sufficiently separate from it."

Guren nodded. "Is there enough for Shinya and the others?"

"There is," said Kureto, opening his coat. Alongside the various assassin's tools and bundles of *fuda* he kept in the inside pockets was an unusual plastic case. Likely it contained more ampoules of the drug.

"So once we take the drug and power up, what do we need to do to be allowed back to Shibuya?"

Kureto reached into his inner pocket again and tugged the end of a slip of paper into view. "I already have your orders. We need to secure power for Shibuya, but someone's in the way."

"Who?"

"A squad of vampires. They're gathering up children. The details are all in here, you can read it later."

Guren nodded.

Kureto stepped closer, holding the syringe in his hand.

Guren glanced at it. According to Kureto, Guren's demon was out of control, but once he took the drug, he would be able to get it back on the leash.

Then maybe he would be able to dispel the doubts that had been flitting through his mind since he awoke: Was he really out of control? Had his demon really taken over? Was this all just a hallucination?

"..."

If he had lost control after killing Mahiru, how could he be sure he wasn't the one who had killed Shinya and the others?

It didn't seem possible. Why would he do such a thing?

But if he was hallucinating, how could he know for sure? He could no longer trust his own judgment. If he really was out of control, he needed to come back to his senses as soon as possible.

"So if I take the injection, I'll be back to my old self again?"

"That's the idea."

"Then what are we waiting for?"

"Right." Kureto made to insert the syringe into Guren's neck, but his hand froze in mid-air.

"What's the problem?" Guren demanded.

"You tell me," Kureto shot back. "Why are you resisting?"

"But I'm not…" Guren looked down at Kureto's hand, only to discover his own left hand gripping it by the wrist. "What…"

"As I thought, your demon has taken control."

"No. It can't be… Stop…." But Guren's left arm seemed to have a mind of its own. "Kureto, quick, give me the shot."

"I'm on it." Kureto flung off Guren's arm and thrust the syringe at him in the same movement. But Guren's left arm moved to block him again. He grabbed his own arm with his free hand—it felt like touching another person.

Not only that, Guren could feel his right arm beginning to lose sensation as well.

"Shit, Kureto, my right arm's also—" His right hand balled up into a fist and took a swing at Kureto's face.

Kureto dodged the blow, but Guren's left arm shot forward of its own accord and grabbed him by the throat. Kureto swept Guren's feet out from under him and he fell heavily to the floor with Kureto on top of him.

Kureto drove the syringe into Guren's neck with the force of his weight.

"Don't fight me, demon!"

The needle pierced the skin of Guren's neck, and he could sense the dark power of the curse churning around the point of injection. It began to worm its way through his body.

"U-Urgh…"

"Control it, Guren. I know you can."

"Ngh…agghhh!" But the curse spread, and spread, and spread. Guren could feel his consciousness slipping away—

The sounds grew muted.

Reality seemed to recede further and further into the distance. Far off, he heard a voice.

"Dammit, it's not working."

It was so far away.

All he could see was blinding white. For a moment, he thought he caught a distant glimpse of Kureto, lifting Raimeiki into the air.

And then there was nothing.

◆

A demon was being born before his very eyes.

A fully rampaging demon.

As he watched, Guren's body began to turn an inky black. He had been unable to bring the curse under control.

"Dammit, it's not working," Kureto said with a scowl.

He lifted his sword into the air and murmured, "Raimeiki."

A woman's voice responded inside his head.

—*You called?*

"Is he lost?"

—*You certainly don't want him to be.*

"Well? Was the experiment a failure?"

—*What makes you think I would know?*

"Then I'll have to kill him."

—*But that isn't what you want to do, is it.*

"It's not about what I want, it's about choosing the right path."

—*Ahahaha! I love the way you tell yourself that, when deep down you're terrified because you aren't sure who gets to decide what's wrong and what's right. Such a coward, and yet so strong.*

"Raimeiki, give me str—"

—*Not so fast, now. The drug is working. Man and demon are detaching themselves from one another. I can feel the demon's presence even now.*

Kureto looked down at Guren where he lay on the ground.

The curse had indeed stopped spreading, and had instead begun flowing back to Guren's neck.

Had he regained control?

"Guren," Kureto ventured cautiously.

"..."

"Guren, are you there? Are you in control?"

At last, Guren answered. "...Yes. Sorry, I lost it for a minute there." He lifted himself into a sitting position and fixed Kureto with a cold stare.

—*That's not him. The drug is working and the curse is receding, but the demon still has the upper—*

"Butt out, Raimeiki," interrupted Guren, almost as if he could hear their conversation. "No one likes a tattletale."

"Are you the demon?" asked Kureto.

The corners of Guren's mouth twitched up.

"Or is that Mahiru?" Kureto pressed on. "Are you alive in there?"

"That's a good question, big brother."

"Are you trying to take control of Guren?"

"Wouldn't you like to know."

"Or is this still Guren, and killing Mahiru pushed you over the edge?"

"Oh no, the drug, it's working! No, stop, I don't want to disappear!"

"Shut up, Mahiru."

"Ahahaha."

"It doesn't matter who you are, you're never getting out again. We've finally developed a drug that will reduce you demons to pets and force you to obey us."

Guren laughed. "Sounds kinky."

—He's right, Kureto, that does sound naughty.

Kureto ignored Raimeiki's needling. Desire was all demons knew. Sometimes it seemed like their one interest was in inflaming human passions, which was why Kureto didn't particularly like engaging with them. He hated the way they could see through to a person's basest desires.

"..."

The drug was beginning to work on Guren.

Kureto could tell, having already taken it himself. It gave the user a huge burst of unbridled power, and then just as suddenly increased their ability to bring their demon back under control.

Naturally, the stronger the control, the greater the trade-off in terms of available power. The challenge in developing the medicine had lain in getting as close as possible to that edge without going over.

And it looked as if it had succeeded in Guren's case. His ability to control his demon was surely much stronger now.

Earlier, Guren said that Mahiru had fused with his demon, but was such a thing even possible? Human-demon fusion was unthinkable within the bounds of their current research, but that didn't mean Mahiru was incapable of it.

The much more logical explanation, however, was that Guren had simply been taken over by his demon, and had lost all reason when he lost control.

Guren had called his demon Noya. That must be who Kureto was dealing with.

Noya had possessed Guren, and shown him visions of Mahiru. In other words, Mahiru represented Guren's deepest desire.

He couldn't save Mahiru.
Couldn't catch up to her.
Couldn't have her.
So he ended up possessed by her.

—*I guess the two of you aren't so different after all. You never could keep up with your little sister, brother dearest.*

That confounded demon. He would shut her up soon enough.

—Mmm, naughtier and naughtier.

"Guren, get ahold of yourself."

"...I'm back."

"Guren."

"Yeah, it's me."

"Hurry it up, Guren, we don't have time for this."

"Ahahahahahahaha!" Guren suddenly burst out laughing. Just as suddenly he began clutching at his head.

And.

"..."

Guren Ichinose opened his eyes, and looked around the room. "...What happened?"

Kureto was standing there in front him. They were in a classroom at First Shibuya High School. Now Guren remembered. He had been injected with the drug.

"I can't remember anything. What did I do?" he asked.

"Your desires took over, but then the drug kicked in," replied Kureto, returning Raimeiki to its sheath.

"Did I...say anything strange?"

"You were pretending to be Mahiru."

"...Mahiru."

"Unless of course you actually were taken over by Mahiru."

"Does that mean Mahiru is still inside me?"

"I already told you, according to our tests the only thing inside you is a single demon."

"..."

"You don't remember anything?" asked Kureto.

Guren told him about the dream he had been having. "I was dreaming again. Mahiru was there, on the other side of the river."

"..."

"Everyone was there, and we were having a cookout. The world was like it used to be."

"So that's what you desire, huh."

"Mahiru just sat and watched. Everyone else was talking, but Mahiru just sat on the bank of the river, dangling her legs in the water. She never said a word."

"It was a hallucination created by your demon. Don't worry, it should be back under control now. Try talking to it, you should get an answer."

"Hmph."

"Do it."

Guren nodded. "Noya," he called.

A voice answered him immediately. "Yes, Guren?"

But the voice didn't come from inside his own mind anymore.

It was coming from somewhere out there, in the classroom.

From the window.

She was sitting on the windowsill, bathed in moonlight—a beautiful young girl, wearing a school sailor uniform, her sleek ashen hair stirring in the breeze blowing in through the broken window. Her legs dangled in mid-air, swinging back and forth just as they had above the river in Guren's dream.

It was Mahiru.

She was right there, sitting on the windowsill.

Guren stared at her.

Kureto raised an eyebrow. "What is it? Do you see something?"

Apparently Kureto couldn't see her.

Then what was going on? Was she real? A hallucination?

Or had Mahiru become a demon after all?

Demons never appeared outside their hosts. Noya had certainly never appeared to him like this.

But in that case, what was *it*?

Had Guren lost his mind?

"..."

"Guren?"

"It's okay. Noya answered me."

"Well? Do you remember what happened, now?"

Mahiru spoke again from her place by the window. "Tell him the Imperial Demons technicians killed me, and you went berserk."

Guren didn't understand what was happening. Was Mahiru really speaking to him? Or was he still hallucinating, tricking himself into believing he heard her voice?

Guren didn't know. Nothing made sense. But he had to do what Mahiru said. What other choice did he have? He wasn't sure yet whose side everyone was on.

And one misstep might spell destruction for his newly resurrected friends.

Preventing that was his only priority.

Fortunately, preventing it was easy. Even if Mahiru was a hallucination created by Guren's demon, it didn't matter. Demons were born of their hosts' desires, and if there was one thing Guren desired above all else, it was to keep Shinya and the others from being killed again. That made following Mahiru's instructions the safest course of action, regardless of whether she was the real Mahiru or just a trick of his mind.

"They...killed her... The Imperial Demons' technicians, down in the lab. They killed Mahiru…"

"And you lost control?"

"Yeah… At least I think so."

"Do you remember anything that happened while you were on the rampage?"

"Tell him you don't," instructed Mahiru.

"I don't remember anything."

"Hmm. Then why did you tell me you killed Mahiru?"

"…"

Guren tried to look like he was thinking.

Again, Mahiru provided him with an answer. "Tell him you felt responsible, like you might as well have killed me yourself. Tell him the demon took advantage of that weakness."

"I…was too weak to save Mahiru," Guren dutifully repeated, feeling like a puppet on a string. "The demon took advantage of my feelings of inadequacy."

"I see." Kureto nodded.

Guren nodded back at him.

"Your response is satisfactory, it's what we expected. The demon is contained. This experiment is now over," said Kureto.

He raised his hand and the classroom vanished. It was yet another hallucination. Or rather, an illusion. The human brain is so easily fooled.

Desire. Despair. Hope. Love. Friendship.

People only see what they want to see.

They were in a laboratory. There were a number of technicians observing them, as well as several dozen soldiers equipped with cursed gear, their weapons trained on Guren. He recognized one of the soldiers as Kureto's retainer. Aoi Sangu, wasn't it?

Guren's friends were there as well—Shinya, Norito, Mito,

143

Shigure, and Sayuri.

Mahiru gestured toward them with a grin. "You see, Guren? Aren't you glad you trusted me?"

Guren ignored her. "Are all these people here to determine whether or not I'm crazy...?"

"They couldn't hear our conversation," replied Kureto. "But if you had gotten out of control, I wouldn't have been able to stop you alone."

He was probably telling the truth when he said their conversation had been private. Kureto had brought up the possibility of rebellion. If word of that got out, he might well be killed immediately. Kureto was too careful for that.

Which meant...

"This lab...?"

Kureto nodded. "Yes, it's my own private facility. The fact that I was able to build this..."

...was all the proof Guren needed that the Imperial Demons' power had waned.

Norito, Mito, Sayuri, and Shigure rushed over.

"Hey, Guren!"

"Guren!"

"Master Guren!"

"Master Guren, are you alright?!"

Shinya sauntered over after them. He looked down at Guren, then addressed Kureto. "Well? How did it go?"

"The drug worked," answered Kureto. "His demon is under control."

"And Mahiru?"

"Dead, apparently. That was the plan, after all. The Imperial Demons had always intended for Mahiru to die as part of their experiment. It seems that witnessing her death pushed Guren over the edge. He even convinced himself that he was the one who had killed her."

"I see..." said Shinya, narrowing his eyes and turning his attention toward Guren. "Must've been tough, Guren. But it wasn't your fault."

Guren looked up at Shinya. His friend was gazing at him with sadness and pity in his eyes.

It was hard to focus on Shinya, however.

Because *she* was standing behind him.

"..."

Mahiru.

That lovely, amused smile never left her face.

But nobody else seemed to notice her.

Was she real, or was Guren hallucinating?

Maybe he really was crazy, after all.

Mahiru raised a finger and put it to her lips. "Shh. Don't be afraid, Guren. I'm real, I promise," his hallucination assured him. Unless she was telling the truth, and she really was Mahiru. "Aren't you glad you did as I said? I knew Kureto would never come here alone. He's so predictable. I'm going to sleep for a little while, now. Good night, Guren."

With that, she vanished as if she had never been there at all.

"..."

Guren stood up and spoke. No one watching would have ever known that anything was amiss. "So we can return to the Imperial Demons now?"

Kureto shook his head. "No, the situation is unchanged. You're traitors. If you want to rejoin us, you'll have to prove yourselves first."

"Prove ourselves, huh. And how do we do that?"

In response, Kureto handed Guren the mission brief and the plastic case containing the syringes. "Power everyone up and carry out this mission. Do that, and I'll vouch for you."

"..."

Guren looked at the case. The drugs were for Shinya and the others. Another drug to make them stronger, at the cost of more of their humanity.

Guren accepted the mission brief, but he didn't open it.

After all, they had no choice but to complete the mission regardless of what it was.

Kureto turned on his heel, indicating that the conversation was over. He gave a few commands to his underlings and began to walk away.

Guren watched him go.

Shinya came up and stood beside him. "Well, well, here we are again, right back under the heel of the Hiragi Clan."

"You're a Hiragi, too," said Guren, looking over at Shinya.

"Silence, knave!"

"Shut up!" Guren yelled back, laughing.

He glanced at the others. Mito, Shigure, Sayuri, and Norito were all looking at him anxiously.

"..."

Guren felt a flood of relief. Seeing them there like that justified everything he had done.

Everything else could turn out to be an illusion for all he cared— he knew his dream of the cookout by the river was too much to ask for—just so long as his friends were really alive.

Guren looked at them and sighed. "Sorry to worry you guys. But I'm back now. Did anything happen while I was out?"

They all smiled and shook their heads.

He knew they were lying.

Their expressions gave it away. Only Shigure maintained her usual poker face. Guren couldn't tell what she was feeling at the moment, but later on he would have to ask what had happened while he was unconscious.

His friends probably didn't want to tell him now because they were still concerned about him. They were kind. That's why he had brought them back. Guren didn't regret doing it, and he felt certain he never would.

Guren stared at his friends, and then looked down at the plastic case in his hand. At the drug that would take away yet more of their humanity.

"You guys…"

But Norito chimed in before he could finish. "We need to power up, right? Don't worry, we know the score."

Mito took the case from him and opened it. There were five ampoules inside, just as Guren expected.

They had to power up.

They had to…

Sayuri spoke up. "Master Guren, we've prepared a room for you. It's late, let's eat and then get some rest. You haven't had a bite since the world ended."

"Sayuri," Guren began.

"Yes?"

"Will you make somethi—"

"I already have, Master Guren," she said with a smile.

"You better appreciate it, too," added Mito, "because I helped."

"Got in the way, more like it," Shigure interjected.

"Hey!"

The whole scene reminded Guren of his dream, of the cookout down by the river. "What did you make? Curry and rice?" he asked.

Shinya smiled. "What if I told you it was corned beef hash?"

"I'd be devastated."

Everyone burst out laughing.

They ate together in the mess hall. As he spooned curry into his mouth, Guren read over the mission brief.

Their task was simple:

Apparently there was a high-capacity emergency power station located in Meguro that the Imperial Demons had owned before the fall, but at the moment it was offline. They had dispatched several squads to the site, but so far none of them, not even the strongest, had returned. Without better intel, the Imperial Demons couldn't afford to waste any more of their troops.

That was where Guren's team came in—their mission was to get the power station back up and running.

There was no plan attached. They didn't have enough information to formulate one. All they could surmise was that monsters or vampires had likely infiltrated the station.

There was no question of whether or not they would accept the mission, however.

They had to.

It was their only way back into the Imperial Demons fold.

Besides, the survival of the human race was at stake. Somebody had to do it. And Kureto would hardly be goofing off while Guren and the others worked. There was plenty to do if they were going to get the city back on its feet.

Everyone had a job to do, and this was theirs. There was no room for discussion. What choice did they have?

They decided to get in a good night's sleep, then head for Meguro first thing in the morning.

Guren ate three full bowls of curry and rice.

"Dude, you sure do like your curry," laughed Norito.

Sayuri was just glad he liked it so much, and Mito chimed in over and over again to remind Guren that she had helped.

Shigure was quiet, and Shinya just grinned through it all.

They wound up injecting themselves with the drug right there in the mess hall. No one lost control. A look of pain momentarily crossed their faces, but then the curse receded.

It was done. Easy enough. And now they were stronger.

This was the world they lived in now. The Imperial Demons would keep upgrading the drug, and they would keep getting stronger and stronger. By becoming less and less human.

Night.

Guren and the others went to their rooms to sleep.

Guren took a shower and changed into a hoodie. There was also new combat gear laid out for him. He would wear it tomorrow on their mission.

He got into bed, but couldn't fall asleep right away. Which made sense. He had already slept for so long. He didn't get back up though, he just lay there in bed and stared up at the ceiling.

At some point he heard footsteps approach his door. There came a knock.

"It's open," he said.

It was Mito. She was wearing some sort of peach-colored pajamas, and her hair was damp, as if she had just come from the shower.

"Can't sleep?" Guren asked her.

Mito stood there for a little while without answering. Finally: "Can I come in?"

Guren didn't know what to say. There was no reason for him to say no. She was his friend, after all.

"Sure," he replied, and in she came, pushing the door shut behind her.

Guren sat up and looked at Mito where she stood in the doorway. She seemed nervous. Nervous, and somehow sad.

"Can't sleep?" Guren asked again.

She shook her head. She looked like she wanted to say something…

"…"

…but she couldn't get it out. She put a hand to the slight swell of her chest beneath her loose pajamas, and tried again.

"…"

But she still couldn't find the words.

"What's wrong?" Guren asked.

"I'm sorry…" she said. She looked ready to cry.

"Why are you apologizing?"

"I shouldn't have come to your room again. We've already been over this."

"…"

"We're…friends… You already told me you can't think of me that way."

"…"

Mito's hand was still pressed to her chest. She was shaking, unable to bring herself to look at Guren. "Everything's changed now, though… My parents, my family, even our followers… I got the report. They're all dead…"

"…"

"I know I'm not the only one who lost family, I know I can't be a baby about it…"

"…"

"O-Only…"

"…"

"I…"

"It's okay to cry," said Guren.

Mito looked up at him. Tears had already begun to well up in her large, round eyes and spill down her cheeks. She was trembling with fear.

"Oh, Guren!!" she cried, throwing her arms around him and burying her face in his chest. She sobbed and sobbed, wailing her lament into Guren's body so that no one else could hear.

She had plenty to cry about. They could try and fool themselves, gorging on curry and pretending to be happy, but the world had gone to shit.

Not to mention the fact that Guren himself was the one who had killed Mito's parents. And now here he was, with his arms around her, holding her to his chest. Who did he think he was, telling her it was okay to cry.

What the hell was he supposed to do in this situation?

What was the right thing to do?

Did he even have the right to touch her?

"…"

Mito was shaking. Guren stroked her hair gently. Hopefully it at least did a little something to ease her pain.

She continued to cry for a while.

Guren said nothing.

Eventually, she calmed down a bit. "…Sorry about that," she said, her face still pressed into his chest.

"It's fine."

"Hey, Guren?"

"Yeah?"

"Is…"

"…"

"Is Mahiru really dead?" Mito asked.

Guren stiffened slightly. What should he say? If Mito realized he was lying, she might be destroyed.

He nodded. "Yeah. I think so."

"Then… I mean, maybe it's not fair of me to ask this, but with everything that's happened…"

"Go ahead."

"If…Mahiru is gone…then do you think there might still be a chance, for me…?"

Guren started to answer her, but Mito cut him off. "Forget it, you don't have to say anything." She pulled away from his chest. Her face was swollen from crying, and her cheeks were red with embarrassment. "I can't believe I cried like that, I'm so embarrassed."

She plopped down next to Guren in apologetic silence, her hands folded in her lap, and hung her head.

Her body—her hips—were touching his.

Guren heard a voice inside his head.

—Oh my god do you want her. You want to ravish her, you think it'll distract you from what you've done. Guren, you dog. Go on, I don't mind. Go ahead and fuck this girl right in front of me, it won't bother me at all.

It wasn't Noya's voice.

It was Mahiru's.

Guren ignored her.

"I'm…not feeling very strong right now…" said Mito. "Ever since that injection, my heart's been racing non-stop."

Demons inflame human desire. They seduce people into letting down their guard and exposing their most private wants and needs.

"I thought I was over it," Mito continued, "that I was fine with the idea of you never loving me…"

"…"

"But the way things are now, we could die at any moment."

"…"

"So what's the point in waiting, for anything?"

—Go on, Guren, give her what she wants. Haven't you hurt her enough already?

Guren ignored the voice.

"Ahh, what am I saying…! I'm sorry. Forget it," said Mito, rising to her feet.

Guren took her by the arm.

"Oh…" Mito looked back at him, expectation in her eyes.

"Mito. Whatever happens, now isn't the time to decide something like this. We just took that drug, so the power of our demons is amplified."

"Oh…right." Mito's face fell. But Guren couldn't sleep with her right now. Not like this. She was his friend. A member of his precious family.

—Is that why you did it with me, then? Because I wasn't precious to you?

Guren ignored her.

"Then, if this had been some other day...you *would* have slept with me?" Mito asked.

"...if you really needed me to."

—Is that what you thought? That I needed your body that day? That I just couldn't live without it?

Guren ignored her.

Mito looked like she was about to cry all over again, but she played it off with a laugh. "Then I guess there's still a chance for me, right?"

"..."

"Too bad my breasts aren't a little bigger," she said, glancing down at her chest and forcing a smile.

Then her face crumpled again, but she powered through, wiping the tears from her wet cheeks. "You know what they say, if at first you don't succeed."

Mito crossed the room to leave.

When she opened the door, however, "What the...?"

For some reason, Norito was standing right outside.

Mito's expression soured in an instant. "W-W-Were you listening?!" she screamed.

Norito shook his head. "Woah, I just got here... Listening to what?"

"None of your business!" Mito shoved Norito out of the way and stormed off.

"Yikes!" Norito stumbled out of the way, flustered. "Mito! Mito, come on! What'd I do?!" he called after her, following her down the hall.

"Leave me alone! We've got an early day tomorrow, go to bed!"

Guren could hear their voices fade off into the distance.

Eventually Norito returned, coming in and closing the door behind him.

"So?" he said, eyeing Guren. "Did you do it with her?"

"No, I didn't do it with her!"

"What's wrong with you!"

"What's that supposed to mean?"

"Her whole family just died. You can hardly blame her for wanting someone to comfort her."

"I'm not sure that would do the trick."

"It'd work for me. I'd rather have a gigantic pair of titties to cry on than a shoulder, any day of the week," Norito confided with a serious expression.

"Dumbass," Guren shot back with a wry smile.

He figured Norito was just trying to lighten the mood. He was the only person Guren could rely on to crack jokes at the end of the world. "Well? What's up?"

"Nothing in particular," said Norito with a shrug.

"Then why are you here?"

"C'mon, I saw Mito come in earlier," Norito protested.

"So?"

"So I was hoping I'd get to eavesdrop on you two doing the freaky-deaky!"

"What, really?"

Norito grinned. "Seriously though, I really don't want Mito to get hurt, you know?"

"You like her, don't you?" asked Guren.

"I dunno. I mean, she's sure pretty."

"Yeah."

"And her personality's pretty adorable, too."

"Yup."

"So yeah, you know what, maybe I do like her. I'm not sure. She's a friend. And we don't exactly have a lot of friends or family left now, do we?"

"Have you found out what happened to your family yet?" asked Guren.

"You know I had a little brother, right?" Norito said after a pause.

"The little brother who's better than you at everything?"

"Yep, that's him. My perfect little brother. I've had a real complex about him ever since we were kids."

"And?"

"I saw his body. He's dead. Stone fucking dead."

"…"

"My parent's corpses were pretty bad, too. That was something. I don't know, there're corpses everywhere now, the whole world's filled with them… I thought I was ready to see the bodies, but when it's your own family, it's something else. Really does a number on you. Like, woah!" said Norito, smiling the whole time. "It's funny. I didn't think I even liked my family that much. It really hit me, though."

It probably hit Norito a lot harder than he was letting on. He'd probably had a good cry. Or if he hadn't yet, he would soon.

"You want to cry on my chest, too?" Guren asked.

Norito smiled. "Did Mito?"

Guren shrugged.

Norito nodded. "Maybe I'll take you up on it too, then," he said. "Just one thing though."

"Yeah?"

"Your tits better be huge!"

"Tough luck!"

"Oh well, in that case never mind."

Just then, the door opened with a click. Shinya peered inside and, spotting Guren and Norito, said, "What are you two doing, hiding out in here?"

"Lord Shinya, you have to hear this," said Norito. "Guren's got a tiny rack!"

"Come again?"

"Why does everyone keep sneaking into my room?" fumed Guren, looking at Shinya.

"I saw Mito come in then leave in tears," Shinya replied.

"How long have you been watching??"

"I was about to run out in tears, too," put in Norito.

"What did Guren do to you?"

"He was about to have his way with me."

"Guren, shame on you!"

Guren rolled his eyes. "Can I please go to sleep now?"

"Well, we found a game console in the common room," Shinya told him. "Come on, let's play."

"We've got an early day tomorrow, th—"

Shinya cut him off. "Tell it," he began, puffing out his chest with a grin, "to someone who cares."

The three boys exchanged glances.

First they woke up Sayuri and Shigure, then they went into Mito's room and dragged her kicking and screaming to the common room. Before long they had the game console hooked up to the TV.

It struck Guren that they were quite possibly the only people in the entire world playing video games at that moment.

Guren Ichinose: Resurrection at Nineteen

It wasn't really an end-of-the-world kind of activity.

Clearly Kureto's other subordinates, stuck at their posts in the laboratory, felt the same way. They looked at Guren and the others as if they were crazy. What kind of person was playing video games at a time—in a world—like this?

They chose the video game version of The Game of Life.

It was exactly what you'd expect: The players were born, they progressed through grade school, middle school, high school, college. They fell in love, got married, and received bonus points at the end of the game for each child they had.

Norito wound up doing odd jobs.

Mito became a housewife.

Shigure worked at a hostess club.

Sayuri became an architect.

Shinya was a musician.

And Guren ended up as a preschool teacher.

Their jobs were assigned by spinning a wheel.

For some reason, everyone burst out laughing when Guren got "preschool teacher." Just imagine!

They wound up playing until two in the morning.

In the end, Mito came in first.

Mito always seemed to win when they played video games.

Even though she was a housewife, she wound up making a fortune through day trading and absolutely crushed the rest of them: at the end of the game, she had 70 billion yen more than her nearest competitor.

"Woohoo! Suck on that! Never underestimate the power of a stay-at-home mom!" she exulted, clearly enjoying her moment.

Guren, meanwhile, came in last. He got addicted to pachinko and borrowed money from a loan shark to cover his gambling debts, had to declare bankruptcy, and ended up divorced.

Talk about a shitty life!

In contrast to Mito, who came in first with a net worth of 70.2 billion, Guren ended up with negative 200 yen.

But at least they enjoyed themselves.

Guren's luck was astonishingly bad. Every time he spun the wheel it landed on something unfortunate. But it was just a game. No matter how badly things turned out, at least the world never got destroyed. Debt or divorce were the worst things they had to look forward to—so spin away!

Once the game was over, they all went back to their rooms.

Guren was glad they had played. Even if they did have to get up early the next morning, playing games together was a reminder that they were still alive.

Before he went to sleep, Guren spent some time thinking about what his life would have been like if he had been born into a normal family, had become a preschool teacher.

What would his reason for living have been then?

Would he have found meaning in watching the children under his care grow up? Or in contributing positively to society?

All of the preschool teachers in the world were probably dead now, though.

All the adults were dead.

What had their lives meant, in the end? And supposing they had survived, what reasons would they have found for living on in this new world? Guren grew sleepier and sleepier as he contemplated these questions, until finally he closed his eyes.

Guren Ichinose: Resurrection at Nineteen

The next thing he knew, it was morning.

◆

Guren and the others were racing through the streets of their ruined world.

The whole city had become an abattoir, and the stench from the rotting corpses was getting worse. If these bodies weren't dealt with soon, sickness would begin to spread.

There were children everywhere, crying for help. But Guren and the others didn't need to stop for them. The Imperial Demons soldiers already had this area covered, and were working around the clock to rescue the children and keep them safe.

The best thing Guren and the others could do for those children was to get the power back up and running.

So on they ran.

It didn't take them long to reach Meguro. With their demonic bodies, they could move faster than a car when they wanted to.

Along the way they spotted a number of the roving monsters. An Imperial Demons combat unit was battling one at the Daikan-yama intersection, in what used to be an upscale part of Shibuya.

"Move out!! Kill the beast!!!"

"Exterminate them, take back our streets!!" the soldiers shouted.

The humans who had survived were clinging desperately to what remained of their world. Despite how bad things were, each and every person was committed to doing what they could.

The monster was strong, and many of the soldiers had already been killed, but the humans weren't about to give up.

Not when the first person was killed.

Nor the fifth.

Seraph of the End

The tenth soldier finally managed to land a blow on the creature's arm.

The thirteenth grappled it and clung to its neck.

And the fifteenth struck off its head.

With that, the monster that had roamed Daikanyama was finally dead.

"..."

Guren and company watched the battle unfold out of the corners of their eyes as they ran past.

Everywhere they looked, the humans were rallying—killing monsters, saving children, burning corpses, collecting car batteries, repairing the streets and setting up camps.

Everyone had a task.

Every surviving human had their own battle to fight.

As they moved through the city, however, Guren suddenly wasn't so sure there was any point to surviving in a world like this.

There was no end to the corpses.

Everything that made the city a city was gone, and in its place only despair remained. There was no way they could rebuild this. The sight was bleak enough to make anyone give up hope.

"Wake up... Wake up...!"

They spotted a small child among the rubble, kneeling next to the dead body of his older brother and crying. The older brother looked like he had been about six; the crying child appeared to be about four.

"Look..." said Mito. "We have to help him."

But if they stopped to help every child they passed, they would never make it to the power station. The same scene waited around every corner.

"I'm sure one of the other squads will help him," said Shigure.

They really didn't have time to stop.

"We have to keep going," added Sayuri, though it clearly pained her to say so.

They were right, of course. They had a mission to complete.

Just then, however, they were interrupted by another sound.

Hweeeeek!

It was the howl of one of the white insectoid monsters. The creature was clinging to the side of a building like a bug scuttling up a tree.

Guren and the others glanced up at it.

"We don't have time to stop and fight…" said Norito.

"But if we don't stop it," Sayuri objected, "it'll kill that child."

"Do you think the six of us are enough to take it down?" wondered Mito.

There was no way to know. They might not be able to defeat it. Earlier it had taken a squad of twenty soldiers to finally kill one of those creatures.

They couldn't risk it.

They had a mission. One that only they could complete. While they were wasting time trying to save one child, Kureto and the others who were waiting for the power to be restored might very well die.

"…Leave him," Guren said. "We have other things to worry about…"

But just then, the monster noticed the child—the four-year-old boy, grieving for his dead brother.

The creature launched itself into the air.

It was obvious where it was headed.

Now was their chance. The monster was focused on the child, and if Guren and the others pressed on, it probably wouldn't give chase.

Hweeeeek!

The monster raised one of its scythe-like appendages as it sailed through the air, dropping toward the tiny, crying child.

"Son of a bitch," muttered Guren, drawing his sword. Tendrils of dark magic writhed over his body as he took off running.

"Guren!" Shinya shouted from behind.

But Guren paid him no heed, throwing himself between the monster and the child.

The beast landed before Guren with a great howl and swung its scythe at him.

He blocked the blow with his sword.

The creature was fast.

Clang. Guren blocked once. *Clang.* Twice. The creature suddenly changed tack. It was no longer aiming at Guren, but attempting to swing around him and strike directly at the child behind.

"Fighting dirty now, are you." Guren swung his sword in a wide arc, somehow managing to fend off the blow.

He heard Shinya, far off, shout, "Byakkomaru, go!"

It was a direct hit. The monster's arms, two of them, were blown clean off its body.

"Alright, here we go," said Guren, adjusting his grip and readying himself. But before he could act, the monster made a slorping sound and vomited a spray of strange yellow liquid.

"Wha?" Guren didn't know what the liquid was, but if he moved out of the way it would hit the child instead.

There wasn't time to grab the kid and run.

What should he do? He had to think fast.

"Shit." Guren spun around and shielded the child with his own body.

The boy looked up at him in shock. "W-W…"

"Close your eyes, kid."

"O-Okay."

The fluid splashed over Guren's back. He felt his skin burning. It was acid. And it was terribly strong. Guren could already feel it beginning to seep into his flesh.

"Master Guren!" Sayuri swung her short sword, slicing off the patch of skin that had been hit by the acid and flinging it away. "Please don't act so recklessly!"

Meanwhile, Shinya, Mito, Shigure, and Norito all rushed the monster.

Guren stood up and rejoined the fight as well.

Even with all of them working together, the monster was strong.

Perhaps because they took their time and played it safe, the battle lasted for a full ten minutes, until—

"Diiiieeeeeeeeee!" Guren struck the final blow, decapitating the monster. Its severed head released one last howl before finally growing still.

They had done it. They had defeated the monster without losing anyone. At their previous power level, it was unlikely that they could have beaten it. But the new drug had worked: they were faster and stronger now. Otherwise, there was no way they all would have made it through alive.

After double-checking that the monster wasn't moving, the group reconvened.

"What were you thinking, taking a risk like that!" shouted Shinya angrily.

"Your wound! Let me see your wound!" cried Mito, checking Guren's back. Thanks to Sayuri's quick thinking, however, none of the acid had penetrated to Guren's internal organs, and his skin had already healed. His uniform had been ruined, but luckily they had brought spares.

"Guys, I hate to interrupt, but if we keep dicking around here we're going to attract another monster. Let's get moving," urged Norito, his eyes flicking anxiously this way and that.

Shigure and Sayuri knelt down beside the frightened little boy.

"Don't worry, you're alright now."

"Everything's going to be okay."

The four-year-old stared up at them, stammering, "Wh-Wh-Who are you guys…?"

Guren looked down at the little boy. "Preschool teachers."

"Oh, gimme a break." Shinya rolled his eyes. "You ended up in debt and got divorced, remember?"

"Huh?" The little boy was bewildered.

"What should we do about the kid?" Guren looked down at him again.

"M-My brother, he's sick," said the child. "You have to help him."

But his brother was already dead.

Guren crouched down and took the boy by the shoulders, looking him in the eye. The kid was crying—tears were still streaming down his face—but he needed to hear the truth.

"Listen to me, okay?"

"But, my brother—"

"Listen to me."

"He got hit by a falling rock. He was trying to protect me!"

"Listen. Your brother is dead."

"No!"

"But you have to keep on living."

"It's not true, it's not true, it's—"

"It is true."

"It's not true it's not true it's not true it's not true it's not true…"

Guren grabbed the boy and hugged him tight. His body was warm—proof that he was still alive.

The boy continued to scream and wail against Guren's chest. "Let go of me! I have to help my brother… He protected me, he…" The boy's voice trailed off into sobs.

"I'm sorry," Guren whispered into his ear. "I'm so sorry."

He meant it, from the bottom of his heart. This was all his fault, all of it.

But he had to convince the boy to go on. "You have to keep on living."

"No!"

"Your brother protected you, it's what he wanted."

"No no no no no."

"Please."

"No!"

"It's alright. You'll be alright."

"Noooooo!!" the boy screamed, but Guren pressed sharply on the boy's back and he passed out instantly. Guren took the unconscious child in his arms.

"…"

Draping the boy over his shoulder, Guren stood up.

Shinya looked on, a sad expression on his face. "Guren…"

"Uh huh."

"We should double back for now, and hand him off to the rear guard."

"Alright."

"But Guren."

"Yeah?"

"We can't help the next one. The longer we take to complete our mission—"

"I know. Sorry."

"No, don't apologize. If you hadn't done it, I would've."

Their other friends all chimed in.

"So would I."

"So would I."

"I would've too."

Guren finally understood how bad things were. *No wonder Kureto looks so awful, he's been dealing with this day in and day out...*

They doubled back, leaving the little boy in the care of an Imperial Demons soldier. When the boy woke up, he would probably scream and cry all over again.

Of course he would. His brother was gone.

And he had to go on living.

In this world.

A world gone mad.

But, what could it possibly mean to do so?

After handing over the little boy, Guren and the others set off running again.

And.

◆

They reached their destination quickly.

The emergency power station was situated down Komazawa Avenue, near the Gakugei University station in Meguro, beneath an otherwise nondescript building.

They encountered no further obstacles on the way there. None big enough to stop Guren and his friends, anyway.

"Strange…" said Shinya. "It's so quiet."

None of the squads Kureto sent had returned—and yet…

They found the subterranean facility easily enough. The generators were damaged and needed to be repaired, but it didn't look like anything they couldn't handle themselves. Sayuri and Norito said they would take care of it. They estimated the repairs would take half a day to complete.

Guren, Shinya, Shigure, and Mito went upstairs to stand guard.

Mito and Shigure were stationed to the east, which they already knew was free of enemies.

Guren and Shinya, meanwhile, were stationed to the west, where they still weren't sure the coast was clear.

They spent four hours together in the building above the power station.

The two passed the time shooting the breeze, talking about stupid stuff.

Anything to keep their minds off the little boy.

And off the carnage they had witnessed on their way there.

They talked about games, sports, the weather. They told dirty jokes. Whatever they could think of to pass the time.

For whatever reason, at some point Shinya turned the conversation to sex. And when Guren asked him why, they ended up talking about why they should go on living.

Because they didn't know anymore. Things were so horrible that they just didn't know anymore, and they naturally ended up gravitating to the topic.

In a world like this.

A world so horrible.

Why keep going?

"With things the way they are, is there really any point to living…?"

"Guren," replied Shinya.

"Yeah?"

"Don't ask me."

"Fair enough."

"I'll tell you what, if you say there's still meaning to life, then I'll say there is, too."

"Chickenshit."

But Shinya just laughed. "Well, make up your mind, Guren. Does life have meaning or not?"

"…"

"Come on, which is it? If it doesn't, I'm gonna off myself, so hurry up and decide already," Shinya said with a shit-eating grin that implied the answer was a no-brainer: it seemed pretty clear he expected Guren to say life had meaning.

"…"

But did it? Guren frowned. In a world like this, was there really any point to living?

No answer came to him.

Maybe there *was* no answer.

Maybe life had never had any meaning to begin with.

But if that was the case, then what were they living for? What was his reason for existence? No matter how long Guren thought about it, he didn't get any closer to an answer.

But what about Shinya, then? Or Norito, or Mito. Shigure, Sayuri, what about them? Or the little boy they had saved earlier— Guren even wanted him to live.

Maybe he was just putting his own ego first, again.

Even if he couldn't find his own reason for living, he still wanted the others to live. And if there was someone who wanted Guren to live just as badly, then maybe he knew the answer to Shinya's question—

"It does."

"Yeah?" Shinya shot back breezily.

Guren desperately wanted Shinya to live. He repeated himself, gauging Shinya's reaction. "Yes, life has meaning."

"That's your decision?" asked Shinya.

"Yup, that's my decision."

How else could he even think about showing his face to Shinya and the others?

He was the one who had brought them back.

The one who had destroyed the world in order to drag them back from the dead.

The one who had decided for everyone, with no regard for anything but his own egotistical desires.

This was the world he had chosen. At the very least, he owed it to them to face up to it.

To work toward a better future.

But how was he supposed to go about that?

How was he supposed to move forward?

As Guren pondered these questions—a voice came suddenly from behind.

—Want me to tell you the answer?

It was Mahiru's voice.

It's not for you to decide, Guren whispered in his head. But she continued.

—I just want to help you.

Bullshit. Are you really trying to tell me you know the meaning of life?

—I do. And I know something else. Shinya and the others only have ten years to live, and I know how you can save them.

You're lying. You're a demon, you're just trying to take control of me.

—I'm not lying. And you're still dancing to someone else's tune. Look sharp now, a vampire's headed this way.

Shinya couldn't hear Mahiru's voice, of course, and he was still chatting away amiably. "It's settled then. So you don't need to worry about it anymore, right?"

"…Yeah."

"And who do you have to thank for that?"

That was when the vampire appeared, just as Mahiru had said he would.

Down below.

There was a man approaching from the west.

A vampire.

"We've got incoming," said Guren.

Shinya saw it too. "I see him. I think I can pick him off from here—"

—Tell him to hold his fire. You need to meet with that vampire, Guren.

"You'll never hit him at this distance," Guren said. "Those creatures are too powerful."

"You're probably right."

"I'm going out there. I'll pin him down, you take the kill."

"Gotcha. And Guren?"

"Yeah?"

"Remember, life has meaning. It's got to. So don't go getting yourself killed."

Guren nodded.

But there was no need to worry. Guren had found his reason for living.

As long as Shinya, Norito, Mito, Shigure, and Sayuri were still alive—Guren had a purpose.

Guren raced out of the office and began dashing down the stairs.

"Mahiru."

"You called?"

"Tell me how to save Shinya and the others."

A grinning Mahiru materialized beside Guren, keeping pace with him as he flew down the steps. "Of course, Guren," she said. "We've got a lot of work to do. Together."

Takaya Kagami here. Nice to meet you.

I say "nice to meet you" since this is a new story arc, but I doubt too many readers out there are actually starting with this book.

This story picks up right after the end of the world.

If you'd like to read about the events leading up to it, please check out *Seraph of the End – Guren Ichinose: Catastrophe at Sixteen.*

Now then, on to the catastrophe in question.

Originally I thought I'd end this series with the last volume of the previous arc. Since it was a story about the end of the world and I had reached that point, it seemed like it would flow nicely into the *Seraph of the End* manga, set eight years later, which is being serialized in Jump SQ.

But then I ended up writing this book.

This is a story about how the human race begins to pick up the pieces after their world is destroyed. I really wasn't sure where to begin, and I also had to figure out what point of view to adopt.

Before I got started, I was scared that it would be hard to make the story of a character who has just committed a great sin and has to face up to that on a constant basis entertaining. After all, unlike

177

with the manga, that sin couldn't be sidelined as a mystery. I would have to constantly depict Guren's own awareness of what he had done. It's a story that begins from a place of overwhelming despair. What was I getting myself into?!

But once I began writing, it turned out to be a rewarding challenge, and I enjoyed the process.

The tale of the catastrophe is over, and now the tale of the resurrection can begin.

Though to be honest, for me, the "catastrophe" of the title was always more about that other keyword—sixteen—than it was about the end of the world. Sixteen—that time in your life when everything still seems so full of possibilities. It was a series about the catastrophic end of adolescence.

In *Catastrophe at Sixteen*, Guren is much more innocent than he is in the manga. He isn't yet carrying the burden of sin.

But Guren takes on that pain, and in so doing becomes an adult. *Seraph of the End* is a tale of two generations: the children's team, represented by Yu and his friends, and the adult team represented by Guren and company. But Guren and his friends lost their childhood. It was destroyed along with the rest of the world.

After the catastrophe of adolescence, what is reborn in people's hearts and minds?

I sincerely hope you'll enjoy this new series.

One last thing: The fact that the manga adaption of *Seraph of the End – Guren Ichinose: Catastrophe at Sixteen* is now being serialized in Gekkan Shonen Magazine played a big part in my decision to write this new series.

The world of *Catastrophe* as depicted by Yo Asami is truly

stupendous, cute, funny, sad—and it helped me rediscover something inside myself that became the driving inspiration to depict the rebirth that follows the end of the world.

If you haven't read the manga adaptation yet, definitely check it out!

And a big thanks to everyone who did read it—the response in the reader surveys was incredible! There was even a huge second run only a week after publication! Hooray!

If everyone spreads the word about the comics and the novels, Kodansha might just get behind a bigger media mix, so I'm counting on you guys! LOL

Okaaay, here we go—a whole new series! I hope you enjoy it!

Takaya Kagami

TAKAYA KAGAMI

This novel is a smorgasbord of scenes that take place on the day the world ends, something I've always wanted to write. I never thought I'd be able to tackle this so directly within the bounds of the light novel genre. I guess *Seraph of the End* is really something...and for that I remain eternally grateful.

YO ASAMI (Illustrator)

I'm a manga artist and illustrator.

I'm currently doing the art for the manga version of *Seraph of the End – Guren Ichinose: Catastrophe at Sixteen*, which is being serialized in *Monthly Shonen*.

The collected editions are on sale too, so please check them out.